I0736703

SINGULARITIES

SINGULARITIES

D.T. Neal

NOSETOUCH PRESS

CHICAGO • PITTSBURGH • MMXXIII

SINGULARITIES
© 2023 by D.T. Neal
All Rights Reserved.

ISBN-13: 978-1-944286-31-6
Paperback Edition

Published by Nosetouch Press
www.nosetouchpress.com

Cataloging-in-Publication Data

Names: Neal, D.T., author.
Title: Singularities
Description: Chicago, IL : Nosetouch Press [2023]
Identifiers: ISBN: 9781944286316 (paperback)
Subjects: LCSH: Science—Fiction. |
Short stories—Fiction. | GSAFD: Science fiction. |
BISAC: FICTION / Science fiction/ General |
FICTION / Short Stories.

Cover & interior designed by Christine M. Scott, clevercrow.com.

Cover illustration, Adobe Stock.

FOR MY BOYS

TABLE OF CONTENTS

The Atomic Baby

THE ATOMIC BABY was delivered by the Stork at 1:30 p.m. CST on April 1, 2112. There was a thump at the door, and I rolled out of bed while Whendee rolled over and murmured in her sleep. I was the light sleeper in the apartment, so when the headphone rang or the cat meowed, or the drunks got to fighting streetside, I was always the one to hear it, I was the first responder.

And I heard the thump and a knock at the door, so I was the one who got up and scratched his head and looked at the clock and went to the door. I thumbed the peephole, got a panoramic view of the hallway, empty, just a hint of baby blue at the bottom of the camera's eye. The peepcam had a wide field of vision, but even it had its limits. Midget gangsters, if suitably close to the door, could evade detection, if they wanted to. I'd heard something about how Biggz Boyz had done just that, routine home invasion kind of things, his pint-sized bravos waiting for the unsuspecting victims to open their doors, ready to bust your kneecaps if you didn't let them have their pick of whatever you had in your apartment. I listened, heard nothing, but stupidly decided to open the door, anyway.

Four locks turned and tumbled and the door was unsecured. I opened the door, and there, at my feet, was a baby in a basket, tucked in, eyes closed, swaddled in blue bunting.

Impossibly cute, like a living doll. When it heard the door latch, its eyes snapped open, and it looked up at me, cooing.

"Da-da!" it squealed, and I felt my stomach do a somersault. I wanted to shut the door, wanted to slam it, to tear my hair out, to scream, but I knew the routine. This had happened before. It had been on the news. The Stork had left us a present.

It was an Atomic Baby.

"Whendee!" I shouted.

The Atomic Baby reached up for me, cooing, looking at me quizzically. It wasn't a real baby. But it was dreadfully realistic, fat little fingers groping for me.

"Whendee!" I shouted, a little louder. It startled the Atomic Baby; the little thing's face wrinkled a bit, it pouted, started to whimper. Its gray-blue eyecams went to red.

"A-HUH!" it said, and I could hear something inside it activating, clicking. I knew what this was; it was on the news. It was a bomb. It was armed.

A tactical nuclear bomb.

I bent down and picked up the Atomic Baby, swaddling and all. It was heavy. Forty pounds? Fifty? More? Heavy little thing. I wondered how many rads I was soaking up just holding it.

"Gah!" it said, smiling uncertainly. It reached out and pinched my nose, hard.

"Ow," I said.

"Hah!" The Atomic Baby said in reply.

"Whendee!!" I said, in a whisper-shout, the kind one delivered when wanting to communicate something very important without making too much noise. With my other hand, I grabbed the basket, carted it inside, shut the door.

There was nothing else I could do; it had been on the news. The Baby had seen me, had imprinted on me. I was its caretaker, hostage, trigger, and victim. If I didn't tend to the Baby, it would detonate.

Whendee stirred in the bedroom. I heard her get some water, swirl it in her mouth, heard the sound of sheets as she tried to get more comfortable.

"Whendee, we've got an Atomic Baby," I said.

"Da-da!" it said, pinching my cheek with pincer fingers.

"Ow!" I said, prying my face loose.

"What?" Whendee asked. I looked at the basket. There was a crisp blue envelope in there.

The Atomic Baby wriggled in my grasp, tried to get free.

"No, no, Baby," I said. I didn't know how atomic bombs detonated, but figured dropping one on my foot was not a good way to go.

"What did you say?" Whendee asked.

"I said we've got a goddamned Atomic Baby here," I said. "Call the police."

"Da-da!" the Baby said, turning, looking in the direction of where Whendee was. "Gah?"

I was sweating, holding the thing, decided to set it down. It thumped on the imitation hardwood floor, looked up at me with its big, baby eyes, and whimpered. I had set it down gently; it just didn't want to be put down.

"Da-da?!" it said, and its eyes turned red again. I remembered the newscasts, when the Stork had delivered the first of them.

"Do not under any circumstances do anything to agitate an Atomic Baby," Foxfire News had said. "If its eyes flash red-red-red, you'll soon be dead-dead-dead."

The Atomic Baby looked at me with red eyes, nurturing a grimace. It held its arms up. I grabbed it and hefted it back up, sat down on the sofa, holding the blue envelope in my other hand.

"We've got a what?" Whendee asked, appearing in the doorway of our bedroom, wearing one of my t-shirts. Her hair was black and sleep-tangled, I could barely see her face. The Baby saw her, turned, trilled at her.

"Ma-ma!" it said.

"Christ," I said. "I told you to call the goddamned police."

"Well, the phone's out here!" Whendee yelled. The Baby didn't like that, yelped in protest, imitating Whendee's tone.

"Don't yell," I said. "Quiet. It likes quiet. That's what they said on the news. It will fucking go up if we piss it off."

Whendee reached up and tucked some of her wild hair behind her ears, her face emerging. Ice blue eyes, oval face, cleft chin, broad lips, straight nose, pale skin, unblemished, unwrinkled—not much touched Whendee. Even life hardly dented her.

"Wow, it looks real," she said.

"Yeah," I said, holding out the envelope for her. But the Atomic Baby wanted her to hold it. It squirmed free of me and clanked up to her, reaching for her.

"Ma-Ma?"

"I'm not your Ma," Whendee said.

"Ma-ma?"

"Just pick it up," I said. "Or get down to where it can reach you."

"I don't want cancer, Dann," Whendee said. "We should just run out the door."

"We'd never make it in time," I said. "Christ, don't you watch the news?"

"Ma-ma!!" it said.

She dropped down to its level, and it crawled to her, grabbed at her curly hair, wound it in its tiny fists. It cooed and giggled.

"Ma-ma!" it said.

I went to the phone and picked it up, but the Baby saw, and carped at me.

"Da-da!" it said, eyes turning red.

"Dann, I don't think it wants you to use the phone," she said.

I put the receiver down and sat down on the sofa, the Baby tracking my movement. I should have walked into the bathroom and told Whendee to use the phone. The news said that if it hadn't imprinted on somebody, its auto-destruct algorithms wouldn't be engaged. I should have hidden with it in the bathroom and told Whendee to call the police, then I'd be the only one who was endangered by the thing.

Its eyes went back to blue-gray, and it turned back to Whendee, tugging at her hair. She bit back on a yowl, trying to get her hair free of its tiny paws.

"Bad Baby," Whendee said.

"Ma-Ma?" it asked.

"No pull Ma-Ma's hair," Whendee said.

It poked at her t-shirt, tugging at the silver necklace she always wore, snapped the links with a yank. The necklace slipped free of her long neck and puddled on the floor.

"Bad Baby," Whendee said, smacking its hand. The Baby grimaced at her, yanked at her hair. Its eyes went red.

"Oh, shit," I said. "Just soothe it. For God's sake, Whendee, just soothe it."

The Atomic Baby squawked, and it began to glow. Whendee was freaking out, nervously singing to the thing in her nice voice, her songbird voice that she used when she was happy. The Baby paused in mid-squawk to listen, then stopped glowing, then its eyes cooled and it was back to normal again, listening to her sing.

"Just keep doing that," I said, "while I read this."

I very quietly opened the letter, to see what that son of a bitch wrote. I know the envelope was basically forensic evidence at this point, but I had to see what that bastard had to say.

Nobody knew who the Stork was; he was a shadowy terrorist, some mad bomber who had ready access to fissionable material and a deft hand with cybernetics. The first Atomic Babies had showed up about five years ago, leading to some unfortunate detonations in densely-packed urban areas, hefty craters, and lots of questions.

The Stork had declared war on 22nd Century America. He delivered his little bundles of terror with seeming randomness. Nobody was safe. It had taken two years before people even realized that the Babies had turned out to be the source of the nuclear detonations. Before then, nobody had thought a portable nuclear device could be deployed in such a tiny package. And certainly, nobody had thought anybody would make a baby bomb. But the Stork had.

Our Atomic Baby was the seventh that had been delivered. Five megatons was what the Stork used. Nobody knew where he got the bomb-grade nuclear fuel for them. No government would admit to it, although in our time, the fuel was sold in various markets, from white to gray to black, to something even darker than black.

"Ma-ma-ma-ma," the Atomic Baby said, watching me and looking at Whendee, who dandled it in her lap.

"It's pretty cute," she said.

"It's a fucking bomb," I said, unfolding the note. The script was elegant, had been handwritten. These days, anything that went through a printer was traceable, and something as old-school as an inkpen was almost unthinkable. But the Stork was a madman, and madmen did unthinkable things.

> *Congratulations! You're now the owner of Atomic Baby Winston. I'm dreadfully sorry to have done this to you, but sometimes one has to use desperate measures to make one's particular point. I'm sure you'll understand.*
>
> *You're probably looking to use a phone, or perhaps your Interweb connection to contact the authorities and send word to them of your situation. I would urge you not to do this, because Winston will receive this very poorly, and will detonate. I've loaded him with a five-megaton warhead that will operate in the usual fashion. I'm sure you're familiar enough with the consequences of abuse and neglect of one of my Babies.*
>
> *Should you treat Winston with care and consideration, however, he will not detonate. I put his fate, and yours, entirely in your hands.*
>
> *Sincerely,*
> *The Stork*

I read the note to Whendee, who stopped dandling the Atomic Baby. The Baby cooed and got off her lap, began crawling around the floor, in a lazy figure eight between Whendee and me. I wouldn't call it by its name.

"That's it?" she asked. "It doesn't even explain why."

"He's out of his mind," I said. "Anything he could say would be so much bullshit."

"We have to call the Metropolice," Whendee said. When the Baby heard this, it stopped in mid-crawl, looked at us in turn.

"Gabagoo?" it asked, its button nose and cherub cheeks the very picture of cuteness. It was an adorable bomb, and it made me afraid.

"Who makes a cute bomb? What kind of maniac?" I asked.

"A crazy one," Whendee said. "They've only defused one of these things, right?"

"I don't know whether they did or not," I said. "They throw out bogus news stories all the time."

I'd even thought the Atomic Baby story was bullshit, until, well, now. I wondered how we would even manage to defuse it. The phone ban was a new thing. Maybe the Stork had responded to the capture and defusing of Atomic Baby Jesus with this innovation.

The Atomic Baby toddled around the room, knocked over a coffee mug that Whendee had left on our coffee table. The mug thankfully bounced on a rug we'd had on the floor.

"Christ," I said, my hands shaking as I grabbed the mug. "We've got to Atomic Babyproof this room!"

I didn't know anything about babies. Neither did Whendee. She grabbed a handful of magazines, put them out of the Baby's reach. I closed doors, picked up pens and pencils, anything breakable. Whendee picked up a pair of socks and a pillow.

The Atomic Baby toddled around, talking to itself. Whendee watched it as she stowed the pillow in a drawer. Seeing her open a drawer, the Baby toddled over, began rooting through the drawer, yanking out the contents, throwing it over its shoulder. Blankets. Little pillows. Whatever else it could find.

Whendee glared at me like it was my fault, like I was supposed to do something.

"What?" I said.

"Look at what it's doing," Whendee said.

"Maybe we can take the thing for a long drive," I said. "They have bomb sniffers in the city, right? Maybe we could get the attention of...you know...those guys."

"Da-da!" the Atomic Baby said, trying to use the open drawer as a step to get to a higher drawer.

"Bad idea, Baby," Whendee said, hefting the Baby off the drawer with a grunt and setting it back on the floor. She closed the drawer. The Baby watched this for a moment, then tugged open the drawer and tried to repeat what it had done again.

"No, Baby," I said. It looked me and bounced a little on the drawer, until I picked it up and held it against my hip, where it squirmed. My arms were throbbing already.

"What if we just left it with somebody else?" Whendee asked.

"No way," I said. "It's imprinted on us. It would go off before we could get away. And it would be wrong, more importantly. Abandoning real babies is bad enough; abandoning an Atomic Baby, even worse."

I couldn't believe she'd even suggested it. We were both sweating.

"We have to call somebody," she said, scratching her head, her hands nervous, jittery-fingered.

"I know," I said. "We're stuck, though."

The Baby had gotten its hands on a nail file and was toddling toward an outlet. Gasping, Whendee went after it, snagged the file, put it on the counter. The Atomic Baby grunted and went into the kitchen, while I struggled to think of how to dispose of this thing, this monstrosity that had come into our lives.

"Stay with it," I told Whendee.

"You stay with it," she said. "You shouldn't have answered the goddamned door! Who opens the door at 11:30 at night, anyway?"

"I didn't know," I said. "Maybe I should take the sleeping pills next time, huh?"

"Hah?" the Atomic Baby asked. It had found a paring knife, was holding it by the blade in its monstrous little hands. Whendee took the blade and dropped it in the sink.

"I'm just saying," Whendee said.

"I know what you're saying," I said. "I wasn't expecting the Stork to hit us. I mean, come on. What've we done to deserve this?"

Did I know the Stork? Did Whendee? I didn't know who his targets were. The Atomic Baby tugged open a cabinet beneath the sink and began rooting around in there, drawing out dish soap capsules which it promptly popped into its mouth, then it chewed on them and spat them out, before finding a puck of steel wool that it clamped down on.

"I bet the closed-circuit cameras in the building tracked the Stork," I said. "He had to come in through one of the entrances. There's no way he'd live here."

Or had he? It was the beginning of the month. Had he just moved out? I wondered what Gretta, the building manager, would say. She had access to the camera tapes. We'd have to notify her as soon as possible, which would be in nine hours, when the office actually opened. That made my stomach clench. Nine hours with a walking atom bomb? It wasn't fair.

"Turn off our headphones," I said. "I don't want some damned telepolitico calling and blowing us up."

The Atomic Baby had taken a bite out of the steel wool, then threw the crescent-shaped puck aside, looking for more treasures beneath the sink.

"You can't just let it play in there," Whendee said, snapping off the phones.

"Why not? It's a robot, Whendee," I said.

"But maybe the Stork wants us to take care of it," she said. "Treat him with care and consideration, remember?"

"It's a goddamned bomb!" I said, and immediately regretted it, because the Atomic Baby was silent a moment, emerged, looked at me with a mix of fear and displeasure. I'd never been stared down by a robot before, didn't know what to do, folded my arms.

"No, Baby," I said, picking it up, closing the cabinet door. I was really sweating then.

"One of us needs to go get help," Whendee said, knitting her fingers as she spoke.

"We should go together," I said. "If we separate, maybe it'll be upset and blow up. It registered both of us. We both go."

The Atomic Baby watched our conversation, its head turning back and forth between us. Could it understand? It had to, despite the Stork's perverse programming, making it act like a baby.

"Maybe we could rock it to sleep," I said. "I mean, the thing had its eyes closed when I opened the door, so maybe it has a sleep mode or something."

Whendee laughed nervously. "You try that, and I'll go get help."

Relationships are about trust, and I had this image of Whendee, my wife of two years, running to the airport and flying away, and me going up in a mushroom cloud.

"Maybe you should try that," I said. "You know, woman, nurturing, all of that."

She looked at me in a way that would have curdled milk. "You know I don't want kids, don't like kids. It seems to like you, Dann. So, why don't you just sit down and rock a little, see if it goes to sleep?"

Great. I came up with the idea, and Whendee delegates for me to do it. I get to rock a fucking atom bomb to sleep. That's love for you.

The Atomic Baby didn't squirm out of my arms this time, just sort of cooed to itself. It was warm to the touch, and I could feel myself getting sterile just cradling that little nuclear nipper in my arms. Back and forth I rocked, using our bungee office chair, which had a tilt-back option. Back and forth, and I murmured a little nonsense song to it, hoping it would go to sleep. I was drenched in sweat as I did this, but the Atomic Baby didn't mind, just settled in.

Whendee watched with some morbid curiosity and genuine affection and admiration. "You're good at it," she whispered.

Care and consideration, I thought. That wasn't so hard, right? Whendee went to our room and she dug out a pair of her black jeans, slid into them, and put on her sneakers and a purple sweatshirt, keeping an eye on the Atomic Baby, which was aimlessly playing with the sleeve of my t-shirt.

What kind of lunatic would make a baby bomb actually act like a baby, I wondered. A certifiably sick son of a bitch, that was who. It was like one of those landmines that activated when you stepped on them, but didn't explode until you stepped off. Claymores? I couldn't remember. They had smartmines these days, anyway. "Smarter than the soldiers themselves." was the slogan I remembered hearing somewhere.

Whendee tiptoed across the living room, past the Baby and me. She got her keys and her wallet, and the Baby stirred a moment, and we both held our breaths, but then it settled into a slumber. She took her headphone and stuffed it into her jeans pocket, then went to the door. Then she reconsidered, snuck back and kissed me, careful to not jostle me too much. My arms were aching. Fifty pounds was heavy if you held it long enough.

"Come back for me, okay?" I said.

"Sure, baby," she said, and crept to the door. She opened it, and the door cracked, and the Baby stirred, but did not awaken. Then she slipped through the door and disappeared, leaving me alone with the Atomic Baby.

It was torture and terrorism, really, I thought, holding onto this thing.

Every time I tried to set it down, it would fuss and fidget, and appear to shift out of its Sleep Mode. What kind of maniac built a bomb that slept? I was really starting to hate the Stork, whoever he was.

I had to pee in the worst way, but was afraid to stand up and wake up the Atomic Baby. I looked at the clock. It was 2:15. Where the hell was Whendee? I imagined her on a bus to Mexico City by now, telling a complete stranger beside her about how she narrowly avoided death, conveniently omitting how she left me in the goddamned lurch.

How hard was it to explain things to the authorities? The Stork was a terrorist. Everybody knew this. Nobody had found the son of a bitch, he was very good at evading detection. People speculated about his identity, like how he was really a rogue government agent, even employed by the government to keep everybody afraid. Like how terrorism wasn't something you left to chance; it had to be undertaken by professionals, who knew what they were doing.

The kind of mind who could create a robot baby bomb was a fucked-up mind, but it wasn't a stupid mind, that was for sure. It got me wondering what exactly the Stork had in mind with his little bomb. That was the key. What was his angle, his agenda?

For somebody with such obvious bomb-making skills as his, he could have simply tacked it to a bridge or a sports stadium, if he'd wanted to make his point. A five-megaton bomb would do an insane amount of damage in a crowded city, leaving a massive crater and thousands of dead, maybe more if it was during a sporting event.

The Stork had already killed something like 150,000 people with his first several Atomic Babies, before they'd successfully defused Baby Jesus. And that was his name for that bomb, not what the Media had dubbed it. The letter had been the same as the one that had been sent to me. The same fucking words, handwritten.

I reached over and took the note again, held it up against the light. I could see a watermark, a stork carrying a baby in its bill. He'd gotten his own fucking watermark, or made his own. The paper was pale blue, baby blue.

Abuse and neglect, care and consideration.

Those were the words that stood out. He was making some kind of political point through the bomb itself, willfully choosing it to be a baby. It seemed plausible—babykillers should die, right? But I had not heard anything like that as a motive in the Intermedia.

Would the Atomic Baby not detonate if I treated it well? Did the other Babies detonate because people didn't treat them well? The first victim didn't have the benefit I did. They wouldn't have realized they'd been handed a bomb, at least until they'd read the note. Assuming the Stork had left a note.

I couldn't remember the name of the first victim, because there'd been so many victims of that first one. Marjury something. It was hard for Metropol to determine who it was, because when an Atomic Baby detonated, it left a crater in its wake, and it was hard to piece together solid forensic evidence in a crater, hard to create a profile. The woman had lived on the 68th floor of the Baldwin Building, and so when it had detonated, it had destroyed that 113-story building and many blocks around it, and because it had been high up, it had spread fallout all over the place, leaving Providence almost uninhabitable.

The Baby stirred, popped a thumb into its mouth. I risked getting up, cradling it against my chest, moving very carefully. I didn't know what it would do if it woke up and found Whendee not there. Would it cry? Would it detonate?

I didn't want to find out.

I went into the bathroom and held the Baby in one hand and peed with the other, not wanting to trust firing blind in the bathroom. The Baby didn't wake up, even as I flushed and washed my hand. Thank Godless.

Going back into the living room, I sat down, and the Baby jostled again.

Abuse and neglect, care and consideration. Those words bounced around in my head, like marbles in an empty bowl.

The Stork wanted me to take care of his baby bomb for him. It reminded me of when somebody would say "Take care of my baby" when referring to some item or object of theirs that they valued, like a car or whatever.

My Baby would take care of me if I didn't take care of it. That was for sure. That's how the others had gotten blown up. They'd armed the things and then had thought it was a prank or a hoax, or worse, they didn't do a good job of it, and the Babies had detonated.

Christ. I wasn't fit to be a father. I wasn't even fit to be a good employee. What did I know about babies, atomic or otherwise? Sure, I'd been one, but I didn't know, didn't remember. My dad yelled all the time. The Atomic Baby was a robot; it didn't need to eat or shit, thankfully. That was something. It needed attention, obviously, and paid attention.

Where the hell was Whendee? She'd ditched me, I was certain of it. I was beginning to get pissed off, even as I was trying to figure out how to deal with this.

I had a Metrocar; it was electric-powered, good for operating within city limits. Fully charged, it could get to the next city, where it could recharge. I could just pop the Atomic Baby in my Metrocar and take it for a long drive, leave it by the roadside, and pray that my car could get me away from it before it detonated. That was a laugh and a half. How far did you have to drive to get away from a five-megaton bomb's blast radius? I didn't know, but I suppose I should have, since it had been on the news, but they'd always measured it in city blocks — like "Another of the Stork's Atomic Babies detonated, destroying one hundred city blocks." What kind of useless information was that? Give me feet, give me kilometers, even! How far would I have to go to be safe? But it wasn't right. That was me simply trying to pass off my problem on somebody else.

I kicked myself for not being able to concentrate, for getting distracted, but I was sleepy, nodding off. I had to keep Baby happy, had to deal with this bad hand I'd been dealt, and hopefully somebody could rescue me. I hated being in that position. Helpless. Like a baby.

No, it wasn't the weapon itself, it was the why of it, the motive of the man behind it. That's what was most important, what I had to dwell on, even as my arms ached.

Assuming the Stork hand-delivered them at all. Supposing he delivered one and it went off prematurely, before he got out of the red zone? Then again, maybe he didn't care. He was out of his mind. Or maybe he'd had some kind of kill switch with him that prevented it from detonating before he was out of range.

My arms throbbed, and I heard the sound of a Metropol cruiser siren somewhere in the distance, echoing in the night air. I heard a drunken couple bickering curbside. Normal city noises. A hovertrain cruised across Lake Michigan, blinking lights of red and green and blue. That was the Nightowl Express, from here to Michigan, last train across the lake. I could see Whendee on that train, could just imagine her, looking over her shoulder, nervous as hell, maybe catching the eye of some late-night playboy with money to burn and looks to spare.

"Dann who?" she'd ask, giving her coyest smile.

And to think I'd even married that woman. Where the hell had my head been? Right up my ass, that's where. I should've left her with the Baby; I'd have gone and come back in twenty minutes, tops.

But had I done that, people would've said "That son of a bitch left his wife with a nuclear bomb! What a bastard!" And she'd have divorced me for it, for sure.

But when the wife leaves the guy behind, it's gallantry, even though Whendee was obviously fucking this up. Women and children first. It was always that. What kind of Victorian bullshit was that? Were they less capable? More worthy?

That thought made me sweat all the more. Where was she? Had she flaked out on me? Maybe they thought she was crazy, maybe Metropol had locked her up, and she was pounding on the door of a cell, telling them that there was a bomb in the city, and they had to stop it. Maybe they'd thought she was the terrorist, a kind of "kill the messenger" sort of thing. Maybe she'd been hit by a car, or shot by a killer clown, or made the sex slave of Biggz Boyz.

What a terrible thing it was to live in fear; it was no way to live at all. It was a living death. I didn't want to die before I'd died; I wanted to live. I wouldn't be afraid. I didn't know where Whendee was, didn't know what I was going to do, but I decided I would do something.

I would not be a victim.

I would not be a hostage.

I would not be afraid.

I got my car keys and my headphone and tucked them into my pocket.

I got up and went to the door of our apartment and opened it, holding the Atomic Baby against my shoulder, and I walked out of there, went down the hallway, passed the silent doors of my sleeping neighbors, thought about waking them up to ask them for help, but decided it was easier just to go into the lobby. I went to the elevator and pushed the button, waited for the car.

The Atomic Baby was seriously weighing me down, now. I didn't think I could hold it and walk with it for very long. I would go down to the curb and I would wait. Maybe a Metrocab would see me, or some late-night revelers.

Somebody.

The elevator came and I took it to the lobby, which was empty, even the concierge having packed it in around midnight. They always kept the lobby nice and cool, which was refreshing. Cool felt like clean to me, and, sweaty as I was, it was a nice change from the stuffiness of our apartment, distracted me from the dread I'd felt.

If I hadn't opened the door, a neighbor might've seen it; it might've seen a neighbor. Then it would've been their problem, not mine. Then again, maybe they'd have boned it up and I'd have been nuked in my sleep, without even knowing why.

I walked over to the concierge's station and took a seat. They had cameras that covered the entry points and the elevators. But I didn't have access to the actual discs. Somewhere on there, there was the evidence. The Stork had been taped delivering this package, and there was still about five hours until I could get at that information. It was very frustrating.

There was a phone on the counter, and it was very tempting to push the Metropol button, the blue shield with the crosshairs on it. The panic button. Would the Baby register that if it was in Sleep Mode? Was it worth risking? I didn't know. It just felt good to sit down.

Where was Whendee?

Bizarrely, it occurred to me that maybe Whendee was the Stork. Or maybe she was in on it. That made me sweat, despite the air conditioning. But I'd have known, right? We'd been married for two years, for fuck's sake. I'd been thinking that the Stork was a guy, but what if it wasn't a guy? Maybe it was a woman? Why couldn't a woman be a terrorist? No reason; hell, a woman had as much reason to be a terrorist as a man, maybe more, if she was really pissed off about something. And Whendee had a temper.

Maybe the Stork wasn't a single person at all. Maybe it was a group.

Like S.T.O.R.K. Strategic Terrorist Organization Robot Killers. Or Suburban Terrorist Operations Resistance Korps. The Metropol and government people had kept us in the dark about the whole Stork thing, it was hard to know what was going on. They never told us anything, just used the mood indicators to color-code our day. "Today is a Red Day. Be extra vigilant, and avoid going out after sundown."

If Whendee had wanted to divorce, she could have just said that, instead of giving me a goddamned Atomic Baby as a parting gift. I'd have understood that.

No, she couldn't have been a terrorist. No way. But part of my brain was nagging me about that, in Whendee's voice, no less.

"Why couldn't I be a terrorist?" she asked, hand on her hip. "I had a life before you, you know. Remember Mark Winston?"

I remembered Mark Winston, her boyfriend before me. Winston. Like the Baby's name. I wiped my hands on my pajama pants. Christ. Mark Winston was this alpha male dickbag she'd been with for about three years before I'd come along. A real shitheel, overtanned, very blonde, tall guy, broad-shouldered. Whendee used to tell me that I wasn't anything like Mark, and that's what she liked about me.

"Mark's all about extreme this and extreme that," she said, tossing her hair. Sometimes you want to just hang out, you know? I like that you just like to hang out. You're like a skinny teddy bear, Dann."

Mark Goddamned Winston. He was the Stork. Yeah.

I was cracking up, for real. My brain was probably being polluted by wayward protons emitted from the Atomic Baby.

No way was Whendee a terrorist. She didn't ever talk about politics; she didn't have any causes more serious than cancellation of her favorite shows on Intervision. I didn't have any causes, either; I just paid attention when I could, which wasn't very often. And terrorism was hard work; Whendee wasn't industrious enough to be a terrorist; she wasn't even industrious enough to be a junkie, or an alcoholic, for god's sake. Terrorism was too much of a commitment for her.

That was the problem with paranoia; like ignorance, apathy, anomie, and fear, it kind of fed on itself; the more you partook of it, the more you needed it to keep going. Everybody was in on it. Yeah. Either everybody was, or nobody was. It hardly mattered; I was the one holding the fucking bomb.

The Atomic Baby stirred, woke up, looked around.

"Da-da?" it asked, squirming in my arms. "Ma-ma?"

"Da-da's here," I said, in my calmest, most soothing voice. The Atomic Baby looked around, head going this way and that. Searching. Noticing.

"Ma-ma?" it asked. "Ma-ma?"

"Ma-ma went out for a bit," I said. "It's just you and me, kid."

It scowled, didn't like that so much, so I tried to distract it, got up, bounced it on my hip a bit as I walked it around the lobby.

"Ma-ma-ma-ma," it said. Where the hell was Whendee? All she'd had to do was get the damned Metropolitical Police.

I decided to go outside, just me in a t-shirt, my pajama pants, my flip-flops, and the Atomic Baby. Out into the sodium lights. The Baby seemed to like that, reached up for them. Good. Pay attention to that, Baby.

There weren't any Metropol guys outside that I could see. No cruisers, nothing. I'd have been happy to see a few snipers, even. Something had gone wrong. Whatever it was, somehow the seemingly routine task of getting a Metropol officer here had not been undertaken.

Natch.

Those guys were always there if you were parked in the wrong zone or were on the street during a protest march. But for something legitimate, a genuine crisis, and they were nowhere to be seen! What was I paying taxes for, anyway? What were we spending all of our money on defense for if some loon could deliver a bomb to my doorstep?

"Ma-Ma?" the Baby asked.

"Da-Da," I said. "Da-Da."

I hated even talking to the thing, even though it was my only company, the only one who understood my predicament, even if it was the cause of it.

Great, Stockholm Syndrome with an atom bomb.

The Atomic Baby looked around, pushed out of my arms, wriggled to the ground, toddled to one of the parked Metrocars. Although I didn't want the thing running loose on the streets, my arms were aching, I was glad to be free of it. I wanted to scream at the top of my lungs. Instead, I stretched my arms, while the Atomic Baby banged the parked car with its tiny metal fists. I leaned against the wall, felt my back crack a few times as I stretched.

"Please step away from the car," croaked the car's alarm, a stern, robotic voice.

"Car?" the Atomic Baby, looking at me with undisguised baby-glee. Then it whapped the car with its fist, denting it, scratching it, and I was in full-on Daddy Mode, rushing to scoop the Atomic Baby from the maroon Metrocar as its alarm went off, a piercing hypersonic screech that startled the Atomic Baby, making it jump back and look at me, ME, of all people, with an accusing face, its red eyes aflame.

"Alert! Alert! Alert!" the car bellowed.

I scooped up the Atomic Baby and ran from the car as fast as I could, the Baby howling in my ear, nearly as deafening as the alarm. I ran a block with it, panting, the Baby hot in my arms, saying anything that came to mind to calm it down. It was impossible to really reason with a bomb, even a smartbomb; they wanted to go off, after all. That was their purpose.

We got to a little enclosed park and playground, long since abandoned. A quiet little oasis in the heart of the city.

"Shh-shh-shhh," I said. "It's okay, Baby. Bad car."

"Bad car!" the Atomic Baby said, wagging a finger over my shoulder at the shrieking car.

"Bad bad car," I said. "Shh-shh-shh."

The Baby's eyes went back to slate blue, and I collapsed on a park bench with it. My hands were shaking. The Baby watched me, then touched my nose with its pointing finger, gave me an exploratory poke. Then it hopped off the bench and toddled around the little park.

It was floored with very old brick, pre-war from the look of it, and was mostly overgrown with vines and ivy. There was a dry fountain in the center, a headless, one-winged angel in the center, brandishing an empty urn that had housed a bird's nest at one time. The Baby clanked around, bibble-babbling to itself as it went.

I dug out my headphone, palmed it, kept an eye on the Baby, which had managed to climb into the fountain and was walking around in circles in it. It didn't look like it was paying attention to me. I was going to take the chance that it had to see me on the phone to react to it.

With a careful flick of my fingers, I turned on my phone, tucked it behind my ear, pulled the microphone to my lips. No messages. Saying a little prayer, I dialed Whendee.

It went to voicemail.

"Whendee, where directly the fuck are you? I can't believe you ditched me."

The Baby patted the angel's feet, looking like a little cherub in some gothic tableau. But it hadn't registered the call. Maybe the Stork had lied about that.

"You're dead to me," I said, hanging up.

I speed-dialed Metropol. A woman's voice answered. A robot.

"Metropolitical Police, how may I direct your call?"

"Bomb Squad," I said. "I've got an Atomic Baby."

"Thank you," she said. "Call forwarded."

A man's voice answered. Another robot.

"You have reached Metropolitical Police Bomb Squad Tactical Operations Officer Jon Barrow. Our regular business hours are 9 a.m. to 7 p.m. If this is an emergency, please dial Star 7."

I dialed Star 7, waited.

Glancing up, I didn't see the Atomic Baby. I looked to my right and to my left, but there was no sign of it. Jumping to my feet, I ran around the park, looking.

Jesus.

A man answered. He sounded weary, bored.

"This is Stiles," he said. "State the nature of the emergency."

"Atomic Baby," I said. "I think my wife, Whendee Olivia Wallace, is the Stork."

"Hold, please," Stiles said. "Patching you through to Telecommandant Fawcett."

"Fawcett here," Fawcett said. "Did you say you had an Atomic Baby?"

"Yessir," I said. "Have. Present tense. It's here."

The man's voice sounded crackly, like he was far away. Probably far outside the blast radius. The Baby saw me on the phone, clambered into my lap, reaching for the phone.

"I need you to stay where you are, Sir," Fawcett said. "Keep the phone line open. We're going to dispatch an emergency rescue team to your location."

The Baby pushed a button on my phone, jarring me. I held the phone up and away from it. Frustrated, the heavy Baby shoved against me, reached for the phone.

"Stop, Baby," I said. "Bad baby."

It looked at me, face full of impudence, or some cybernetic facsimile of it. Okay, so maybe the Stork had lied about the phone thing. Thank Godless.

Two trucks rolled up. Both Metropol trucks, squat and black, with white stripes across them. They looked like giant skunks. I'd never seen them up close. If Metropol came for you, you were in big trouble. Out came a half-dozen Metropol officers, dressed in body armor and helmets with mirrored visors, carrying assault rifles. What that armor would do against a baby nuke was precisely nothing, but they looked impressive.

I hefted the Atomic Baby and let it rest its heavy chin against my shoulder. I didn't want it to see the men. It squirmed in my arms, cooed.

One of the Metropol officers had some kind of device held out in front of him, a little box. He was reading it.

"Yes, it's him," he said aloud.

"Sir, we're going to ask you to come with us," another Metropol man said. The Atomic Baby squirmed, tried to turn around to see the men.

"No, baby, shhhh," I said. I didn't want it to be scared. God, no. "Okay, but you got my message about Whendee, right?"

"Yessir," the officer said. "It's all been recorded. We got it. We'll find her, don't worry."

The Baby whipped around and looked at the policemen, making everybody flinch. It pointed at them. "Bang!" it said, reaching for one of the officers' rifles.

"We're going on a trip, Baby," I said. "Right?"

"Yes," one of the faceless officers said. "Get in the back, Sir."

"Me, too?" I asked. It didn't feel like an emergency rescue, versus, say, a special detention. Everybody knew that if the Metropolitical Police detained you, that was it. You just vanished.

"Yessir," the officer said. "Standard procedure."

"Where are we going?" I asked.

"In the truck, Sir," the man said. "That's where we're going."

I climbed in the back, and the Baby looked around, cooing with interest, trying to grab at the inside walls of the truck. It looked like one of the riot trucks Metropol would use. I didn't know, had never been inside one.

The men closed the door, none of them joining me in the truck, and I heard the truck start up and away we went.

"What the hell?" I said, going to one of the armored windows. Another Metropol truck was following us.

"Truck!" the Baby said with glee, banging on the smoked glass with its metallic paw, making a clinking sound that apparently delighted it, for when I moved away from the glass, the Baby became angry, forcing me to return to it.

There were no handles on the inside of the door. I was trapped with my baby bomb.

"Where are you taking me??" I called out.

An intercom crackled. "Please stay calm, Sir. We're moving you outside of city limits, for safety reasons."

"You guys were supposed to rescue me," I said, while the Baby squirmed out of my arms, toddled along the floor with hefty clanks. "This is bullshit."

"Bullshit!" the Baby said, clapping its hands. The truck hit a bump, and the Baby pinwheeled its arms, fighting to stay on its feet. Then it clanked onto its bottom. A toddling bomb. The Stork was a lunatic.

"Please remain calm, Sir," the voice said. "We're taking you to a secure location."

"What about Whendee? She's the Stork!" I said. I didn't really know, but it was pissing me off so bad how she'd left me hanging in this.

"Whendee!" the Baby said. "Mama? Mama!"

"I want to call a lawyer," I said.

"You haven't done anything, Sir," the voice said. "Why would you need a lawyer?"

The accusation implicit in that question quieted me for a moment. It would be okay. They were just taking precautions. Couldn't defuse a nuclear bomb in the heart of the city, right? It only made sense.

"I just opened the door," I said. "It was there."

The Baby looked at me, smiled, then went to the wall of the truck, rapping with its pudgy metal fists. The truck had two benches on either side of the truck, lightly cushioned in gray polyfoam. The truck's interior was white.

We drove for awhile, and then stopped.

"What's happening?" I asked.

"Another pickup, Sir," the voice said.

I could hear a muffled commotion outside, went to the smoked windows, but just saw the Metropol officers carrying a struggling person. One of them came to the door, and almost reflexively, I flinched away from it. The door came open, and the Baby turned and looked with delight, then began walking toward the door.

The Metropol officers bodily handed Whendee into the back of the truck, while she was spitting and cursing at them.

The doors shut.

"Mama!" the Baby said, toddling up to her.

Whendee's eyes were wild, fierce. She got up, banged on the doors. "Let me out! Let me out of here, you fucking nazis!"

The Baby imitated her, banging the door with its fists.

"Hey, there, Whendee," I said. "Small motherfucking world, isn't it?"

She whirled around. "You ratted me out, you bastard! I cannot believe you gave my name to Metropol."

"I can't believe you ditched me," I said. "Tit for fucking tat, as I see it."

"You said I was The Stork," she said.

"Well, are you?"

"No," she said, her face wrinkled with contempt. "Do I know how to make a bomb? Let alone some fucked-up robot baby bomb? Come on, Dann. Don't be stupid. Just for once, don't be stupid."

"You ditched me," I said.

She didn't even really look guilty; just really pissed off.

"It's a bomb, Dann," she said. "I was trying to get out of town. They nabbed me at the train station."

"Thanks, baby," I said. "Really. Thanks a lot."

The truck started again, and away we went. We drove for hours, Whendee on one side, me on the other, the Baby toddling between us, our little nuclear family, together until Armageddon.

Timekeeper

YEAR ZERO

STRAWN DIDN'T tell anybody. He had made the time capsule, a device of his own design, and he hadn't told anybody about it. To tell was to ruin everything, and so he didn't. He filled the capsule with a variety of things he thought might be of interest to the future: a bottle of red wine, a bottle of whiskey, a bottle of brandy, and a bottle of cognac; his memoirs (he hadn't done anything of note—rather, it was his life's story to that date); a personal letter from himself to the future; several news and cultural periodicals from the day, protected in plastic baggies; some hair clippings (both current and from his baby book); transcripts of several popular songs (he had thought about putting in discs, but figured they would be devoid of charge by the time they were discovered); pictures of himself, of his ancestors, of his family; some catalogues; a handful of coins, including some gold ones from that year; a vial containing gasoline; several toy cars featuring contemporary designs; a cellphone (in a baggie); he'd made predictions for the world, thoughts and feelings he had about it (something future generations might find amusing); he included several books, and that was almost the toughest part, because what did one settle on? He figured enough capsules had the Bible in it, so he went in another direction: the complete works of Shakespeare, a few anthologies of literature, a coffee table book about the Minoans, some MAD Magazine reprints. It was a personal thing for him.

Most importantly, he'd put the Chronometer in there. He distinguished it from a watch because its purpose wasn't to tell time, so much as to track the passage of time, and to serve as a beacon. He'd made the thing with a chip of Americium in it so that it would last for a long, long time. Many fire detectors had perished in his quest to build the Chronometer.

Strawn didn't relish making something radioactive, so he was careful about sheathing the capsule in lead and stamping a warning on the surface of the thing. He set the Chronometer with a touch of two buttons at opposite ends of it and watched it click to life, tracking seconds. Then minutes. He'd left ample decimal places for it, using special carbon silicate wafers he'd fabricated...

000,000,000YEAR:000DAY:00HOUR:01MIN:30SEC

He hoped it would be enough time. With each tick of the Chronometer, the thing gave off a pulse, a radioactive samba that he hoped would be detected by future generations. Strawn wanted the thing to be found. More than anything.

So, with the Chronometer running, he put it in its little box and put that on the outside of the capsule, like a warhead in the bullet-shaped thing. The Chronometer fit snugly, and then he sealed it in its titanium shell, and he hoped it would be enough.

The capsule was sealed and Strawn decided where the best place to put it would be. He didn't want somebody stumbling on it and thinking it was a bomb. The thought of a tactical police unit robot detonating his time capsule made him ill.

But it mattered where he put it. It needed to go someplace undisturbed. Strawn had really wanted a salt mine, but he lacked the means to acquire one, so he fabricated one in his backyard, digging in a place where he thought nobody would disturb it, and then lining the hole with three steel-ply plastic trash bags, and then packing that bag with rock salt. He nestled his time capsule in that bed of rock salt and finished filling it up. Then he burned the bag shut with an electric sealer, so there would be no seams in the bag.

After that, Strawn mixed and poured concrete into the hole, and leveled it off, stamping "2011 AD" on the concrete. After a day, that Quickcrete block had set, and then Strawn covered it with dirt.

He took out his scanner and checked it. The Chronometer's pulse showed up, and Strawn felt satisfied that his little capsule could be recovered at some point by folks from the future. Very pleased with himself, he put the scanner on his work desk and treated himself to a beer.

Later, Strawn went to the mail and checked it. Bills. Bills. Solicitations. A box. He gave the box a shake, but nothing thumped in it. There was no return address. It was the size of a cigar box. Strawn took it back upstairs to his place and opened it.

Inside was a pale blue envelope with his name written on it in gold script, and the Chronometer. Strawn's heart skipped three beats as he gazed at the thing.

000,000,001,929YEAR:300DAY:33HOUR:13MIN:28SEC

The second hand ticked away. Strawn grabbed his scanner and he checked it. It registered two Chronometers. In the backyard, and in front of him. Paradox. Time travel.

He'd fainted before even reading the letter. Fell flat on his face.

THE LETTER

First the sound came back, and then the tightness in his stomach, and then, at last, he could see. As it happened, he'd fallen near the Chronometer, which sat on the floor, facing him.

000,000,001,929YEAR:300DAY:33HOUR:20MIN:11SEC

Strawn saw the letter, crisp and clean, and reached for it with sweaty, shaking hands. Addressed to him. Turning it over, he saw a gold blob of sealing wax on the envelope. The thing wasn't made of paper. At least nothing he recognized. He gazed closely at the seal.

The writing was unrecognizable, but the symbol was an hourglass turned on its side. He could see that clearly enough. Strawn set the envelope carefully on the desk, and poured himself a drink, taking a swig of brandy. Then another.

He hadn't told anybody. Nobody had known.

How had it gotten here? He'd hoped that the Traveler would have visited in person, not sent some stupid letter. Not that a letter was stupid; he liked letters. But he'd wanted something more grandiose, more futuristic. A letter was so retro. And a letter almost 2000 years from the future was beyond retro; it was almost insulting, condescending.

And yet, he had to consider himself fortunate to have received anything at all. It meant that there was a future of some sort, and that felt gratifying to him, knowing this little-huge secret. Time travel was possible in the waning days of the year 3940 AD.

Still, why had the person or persons bothered to write him at all? He'd wanted desperately for them to visit him, but he knew that they knew the inherent risk of such a move. It was a cliché, the perils of visiting the past, of changing it.

But there was this letter, and his Chronometer, still tracking the time. He felt stupid for letting it go on counting; he should have turned it off when he'd first opened the package, but he'd been too shocked. So, belatedly, he shut the thing off:

000,000,001,929YEAR:300DAY:33HOUR:25MIN:01SEC

"Better late than never," he said aloud.

Strawn took the letter and held it to the light. But while the letters of his name caught the light and toyed with it a bit, the envelope, for all its thinness, was not translucent.

He wondered how the Traveler had delivered it, looked back at the box. It was postmarked with yesterday's date. That made him smile. The letter from the future arrived a day ago. Just thinking it made him dizzy.

Was the Traveler in town? They had to be. Strawn hadn't known what to expect. A glamour goddess in silver thigh-high boots and a plexiglass bra, her pink hair teased up around her head like a nimbus. Perhaps a sleek robot, or a cyborg, a tech-savvy visitor warning him away from his present course. Anything was possible in the future.

Carefully, Strawn opened the envelope, breaking the gold seal. He thought it was funny that they still used sealing wax in the future. Or, perhaps it was another extratemporal nod to the ancient past on the part of the Traveler. Something to make him more comfortable.

Inside the envelope was a sheet of paper, ivory colored, tri-folded. He took it out and opened it.

The page was blank.

"What the hell?" Strawn said, turning it this way and that. There was nothing written on the page. He looked back at the box, saw where it had been routed. East Thalerton.

That was right. The Traveler knew where he lived, and when. But to send a blank letter? What was the point to that?

Then Strawn thought that maybe there was a secret message on the note. He went to the window, held it up to the light. Light did pass through the paper, but there was no message that he could see. He didn't want to subject the paper to any rigorous treatment, for fear of damaging or destroying it.

Strawn went back to the envelope, looked inside it for anything. It was empty. His excitement corroded into despair.

Something occurred to him: perhaps the letter itself was the message. The Traveler might have been wary to alter the past too significantly, so they just sent him the blank letter to let them know that they had received his capsule.

"But I wanted to talk," he said, feeling utterly rejected. The writing on the envelope looked like that of a woman's hand, and Strawn had wanted to meet this Traveler. He couldn't believe they had snubbed him that way.

THE PARADOX

Strawn wondered what would happen if he dug out the time capsule and put the two Chronometers together. He'd read that it was impossible for two of the same thing to occupy the same space. What would happen if he'd held the same Chronometer in different hands?

He didn't relish digging up the time capsule, but it nagged at him. He held the future Chronometer, which looked very old in his hands. And scarcely 30 feet away was the same Chronometer, ticking away.

But then he wondered if doing that would then tamper with the future. He assumed that it would. Since he held the Chronometer in his hand, obviously he hadn't dug the thing up. Or else he'd dug it up and replaced it again.

At what point did volition become destiny?

Strawn wished that the Traveler had come. It would have made all of this unnecessary. If he dug up the capsule, maybe something would happen that would prevent it from being discovered by the Traveler. Could the Traveler see him now?

He looked around him. There were some willow trees, hanging heavy over his yard. The neighbor's weathered transwooden fence. On the other side, the neighbor's steel shank fence. Strawn couldn't see anybody.

The Chronometer sat lifeless in his palm. He'd really not expected the thing to last as long as it had, but had been pleased that his design had aged well.

000,001,929YEAR:300DAY:33HOUR:25MIN:01SEC

It was history he was holding, though nobody else would realize that, or think it. Although if a scientist looked at the Chronometer, they could surely determine its great age. The Chronometer itself was proof of time travel.

Not enough. He wanted to hold the paradox in his hands. He went to his toolshed, unlocked it, and got out a pick and a shovel. It pained Strawn to think of digging up his beautiful time capsule, but he assumed he could just replace it. The Chronometer was readily accessible. That was its purpose.

He went to the burial site and he removed the dirt and got to the 2011 AD and cracked it with a couple of blows from his pick. Then he widened it with a few turns of his shovel, until he got to the trash bags. Strawn then tore those open, rock salt spilling out, and saw the Chronometer ticking away.

000,000,000YEAR:002DAY:11HOUR:16MIN:01SEC

Strawn unscrewed it and held the thing in his palm. Then he looked over at the other one. And it was still there. Sweat poured out of him, both from his exertions and from the monumental weight of what he had before him.

Holding the original Chronometer in his left hand, Strawn picked up the future one in his right. How could it even be? The present, past, and future were in his hands.

What he had done had not changed anything. Not yet. Perhaps in the near future he replaced the capsule in its burial site, after playing with the Chronometers.

Then something occurred to him. Perhaps the Traveler wanted him to do this. It could, perhaps, explain why the Traveler had bothered to contact him at all. Maybe the Traveler wanted him to change the past.

Strawn held the Chronometers in front of him, watching one tick and the other stand still. Nothing had happened. Nothing could happen if they came together, because they couldn't occupy the same space. They could touch, but it wasn't the same as occupying the same space. Strawn didn't see much point in having them touch each other, but the idea of it made the hair on his neck stand up. How many people had held impossibility in their hands?

He thought about replacing the current Chronometer with the one from the future. That was amusing to him. A little joke on the future. Laughing, he did just that, screwed the future one into place and repeated his careful ritual with the time capsule, burying it again.

THE TRAVELER

Of course, as he walked around East Thalerton, Strawn couldn't help but wonder if the Traveler was there, watching him. He evaluated each face as he went through his daily routine: stopping by the store to pick up some groceries, he looked at the other shoppers, wondering.

An old woman with her tanned Oceanian handler piling boxes of silken tofu into a motorized cart. A lone teenager with hair lacquered into a great emerald spike, like an antenna. The teen walked back and forth, watching himself be tracked by the security cams. These folk didn't seem like the Traveler to him.

Walking down the street, Strawn tried to think what a Traveler would even look like. Depending on the historical records, like how thorough they were, a Traveler would likely try to fit in as best as they could. As he worked his way along the cracked sidewalk, avoiding spars of broken concrete, Strawn wondered if East Thalerton seemed exotic to the Traveler.

The crumbling buildings and the security fences didn't seem so exotic to him, but he'd known them all his life. His work kept him safe in town, or relatively safe, so long as he was in before curfew. But as he sniffed the ethanol-stinking air, he thought perhaps the Traveler might think his home was frightfully barbaric.

He went to Squeeze's House of Juice and got himself a bottled beverage (synthgeneered gooseberry cola) and drafted his note to the Traveler.

Dear Traveler—

I received your cryptic reply, but can't help but wonder why you didn't pay a visit, or at least drop me a line or two. I had really hoped to meet you, as was made plain by the original note I wrote, explaining the reasons behind the whole enterprise.

Hopefully, you'll reconsider and drop by, so we can talk. I know this is probably an unconscionable breach of temporal etiquette, or perhaps an act of hubris, but I'd love to know what your world is like, and what you are like.

Regards,
Jon Strawn

P.S. I certainly hope my little action with the Chronometer didn't cause any dire consequences.

He sealed that note into an envelope, and finished his drink. After doing that, he went home, sealed the envelope in a plastic bag, put that bag in a waterproof box, placed the box into a protective transalloy cannister, and then buried that in his backyard, next to the original capsule.

After burying the cannister, he realized that he'd forgotten to check the mail, so he went back out front, dusting himself off.

There was a letter there, postmarked for East Thalerton from the day before. How could he have missed it? He realized with a grin that he hadn't missed it. It simply hadn't existed the day before. The Traveler had left it for him.

THE REPLY

Strawn washed his hands before reading the letter. Then he poured himself a drink, and sat down with the letter, which was itself sealed carefully in a packing envelope. He tore it open and out came a blue envelope, with his name scripted on it in gold, and on the back, the blob of hourglass sealing wax.

He opened it without hesitation this time, and out came the weird non-paper he'd seen the other day. Strawn laughed—he'd lost track of time. He glanced at the Chronometer, only to discover that it was gone.

Jumping up, he looked around, seeing if maybe it had fallen on the floor, but it hadn't. The thing wasn't there.

Strawn opened the letter with a shaky hand, and was pleased to see writing on it this time, in that same delicate script.

Dear Mister Strawn—

Sorry about the non-contact. Regulations are terribly strict about extratemporal incursions. Of course, I'm already in deep trouble for initiating a correspondence at all. As you can see, I am a scholar of ancient languages, and think I am doing rather wall, wouldn't you agree?

Thank you for the delightful grifts you sent. The brandine in particular was criminally good. I hope I used that properly. At any rate, it sounds like you live in a very unusual time. Rest assured that I won't spill the bones about the future.

With regard to actually meeting one another, I think that can be arranged. I have run it by the Consulate and since you are already temporally compromised, it seems unlikely that there would be any paradoxical problems associated with a brief moating.

You name the time and place, and I'll be there.

Temporally yours,
Evanthia Wayward

P.S. As for your prank with your timepiece, I took preventive measures. Paradoxes are prohibited by law. Look on your furorplace mantle. Don't do anything like that again, please!

Strawn saw the future Chronometer, sitting on the mantle. He went to it and looked it over.

000,001,929YEAR:300DAY:33HOUR:25MIN:01SEC

Evanthia had replaced it, alright. He couldn't believe he hadn't noticed it before. But when had she done it? He ran to his back window, looked out the back. Nothing looked disturbed to him. Had she done it this morning? It hardly mattered to a Traveler. They had all the time in the world.

He poured himself another drink and jotted another note, first thinking Squeeze's might be a good place to meet, but then settling on something more elegant: Fine Restaurant. The Fine Restaurant chain had been started a few years ago by entrepreneur Frank Fine, who was interested in franchising elegant dining experiences. It seemed the perfect place to stage such a rendezvous.

Not that he was planning anything exceptional. He just thought an ambassador from the future deserved the best he could offer.

Evanthia Wayward. It was a pretty name, as elegant as her writing. He'd hoped for a hologram, or something more technologically advanced, but he assumed she was dumbing her correspondence down for his benefit. He liked the various errors in her syntax—they were oddly endearing. He didn't know if it was presumptuous of him to correct her on those. He wondered if his East Thalerton accent would be off-putting, or what she would sound like.

He wrote a time and the place (gave himself three days to get ready, hoping that he wouldn't be hit by a bus in that time, or be shot, or die of a heart attack), and ran out to Jiffy's Hardware to get another transalloy cannister, mindful of everything and everyone around him. The ground seemed to sing, the air was sweet, the clerk was sour ("Another cannister? What you got over there, Mister Strawn?"), but life was good.

Strawn whistled as he tucked the letter into its secure little transalloy case and buried it in his backyard, along with the others. Then he ran to his mailbox, breathless, as the mail carrier drove up.

"Expecting something?" the carrier asked. His name was Stew. He was ten years younger than Strawn, and his lip ring trembled a bit as he talked.

"I sure am," Strawn said. Stew dug through his bag, feigned surprise, held up an empty hand, turning it this way and that, as if he'd done a magic trick.

"Nothing today, guy," he said, driving away on his scooter, cackling as he went.

Strawn felt crushed. Then he thought to look in his mailbox. And there, inside, was another envelope, postmarked from the day before. Strawn snatched it up and ran back inside, laughing aloud.

THE MEETING

It wasn't a date. This Strawn told himself as he bought flowers and a new polyflannel suit. This was a summit. A historical meeting. And yet, he couldn't wait to meet Evanthia. He'd written out questions to ask her, hoping that he would not make a total ass of himself. Strawn had never been so excited in his life. He doubted he would ever be that excited again.

He worried that he'd appear too rustic, too provincial. For somebody from the future, he tried to imagine talking to someone from the Year 1000, like how different they would be from him. Of course, he'd have almost nothing in common with someone like that, and that's how Evanthia would see him. Historical curiosity; an anthropological specimen. A relic.

Maybe she was a student, working on a dissertation, or whatever passed for it in the future. He just didn't know. She knew everything about him that he'd put in that time capsule, but he'd known nothing about her. So he was definitely at a disadvantage.

Strawn got to the restaurant early, wanting to be sure to have a good booth. Every seat in Fine Restaurant was a booth, every one clad in crinkly red syntholeather, with low lights. Tasteful, understated music played on the unseen speakers, and somewhere, a fountain burbled.

As he sat in his booth, with a commanding view of the floor, Strawn ordered a Manhattan and waited for Evanthia to arrive.

Each time he saw someone cross the richly carpeted floor, he thought *Is that her?* With a mix of disappointment and chagrin when it appeared not to be her. Waiters and waitresses hustled by, looking sharp in their white tux shirts and black ties and crisp black slacks. His own waitress was a tall, attractive-looking young woman who looked almost like a young Roma, with black hair and a prominent, straight nose and wide-set eyes.

He glanced at his watch. It was 8:08. She was late, but still fashionably so. Sweat nipped at the back of his neck as Strawn contemplated being stood up. It hadn't happened before, but Strawn hardly ever dated, thus minimizing the risk.

The flowers he'd brought were roses; sky-blue. He thought she'd like those, because of her choice of envelopes. He didn't know, so he just winged it.

The waitress showed up again.

"Another drink, Mister Strawn?"

"Uh, sure," Strawn said. She set down a Manhattan on the table, then sat down in his booth, holding out her hand. "Evanthia Wayward."

Strawn gawked at her, then shook her hand. It was strong and cool to the touch. Evanthia smiled at him, an altogether becoming thing. She was enjoying her little prank.

"You got a job here?" Strawn asked, staring at the holographic candleflame that flickered on the center of the table.

"I've been working here for a month," she said. "Once I saw that's where you wanted to go, I thought I should check the place out, get a feel for early 21st century mass-marketed pseudo-luxury dining."

Her accent was very unusual to him. He had no words for it. The idea that she'd been here for a whole month made him grimace. She'd been here before he'd even buried the time capsule. He'd eaten at Fine Restaurant in the past month. He hadn't even seen her.

Her eyes were the color of dirty moss.

"You've been working as a waitress?" Strawn asked. Evanthia nodded.

"Research," she said. "This place burns down in another month, so there's no problem with displacement of indigenous labor. Whoops. I wasn't supposed to tell you about the fire."

Strawn couldn't tell if she was joking or not, so he slid the flowers across the table to her.

"How pretty!" Evanthia said. "Really prime."

She reached out and pricked her finger on the thorns, yelping as she did so.

"Hey, they bit me!"

"Thorns," Strawn said. Evanthia daubed her long, slender fingers with a napkin.

"Bred out of roses in 2038," Evanthia said. "Whoops. Wow, that really stings."

Strawn didn't like to think that Fine Restaurant would be up in flames in a month's time. He liked their food. Evanthia watched him while she finished nursing her fingers.

Something popped into Strawn's head. "You aren't the one who burns this place down, are you?"

Evanthia cocked an eyebrow at him, an elegantly trimmed and shapely thing. "Everybody is so paranoid around here."

Strawn felt embarrassed, sampled the drink. It was perfect. Evanthia seemed pleased by his reaction, and Strawn felt like he had to say something, so he did.

"So, are things better in the future?" he asked, biting his tongue, feeling lame.

"Worse," Evanthia said. "You have no idea. In fact, part of my research project is to find the causes behind some particular effects that have been plaguing us back home."

"Are you on a mission?" he asked. He could see her as a lady spy. She had a feline grace to every move that Strawn imagined spies as having, though he thought actual spies were probably more ratlike than catlike.

"No," Evanthia said. "Nothing so romantic as that. Or creepy. Just research. I can't tell you enough how prime it was to find that time capsule of yours. We thought it was some postwar wreckage, like a mine or a bomb, and then we saw what it was. I could go on and on, but this is supposed to be about you, Mister Strawn."

A plate of food arrived, surf and turf, one of Strawn's favorites. He knew better than to ask how she knew. She must've seen him order it. Or had he mentioned it in his time capsule memoirs? He couldn't remember. Perhaps she'd seen him eat it elsewhere. He supposed one could access credit records readily enough as a means of tracking time and place.

Evanthia ate a great big pork chop, cutting into it and devouring it with gusto.

"I thought you'd be a vegetarian," he said. "I mean, overpopulation and all."

"It's so good," she said. "I miss pigs. Whoops."

"Pigs are extinct?"

Evanthia took a guzzle of water, wincing at the taste. "Mmmmaybe."

"Well, either they are or they aren't," Strawn said. "Cows I can see."

"Cows are sacred," Evanthia said. "You have no idea. Look, you can't keep grilling me about that kind of stuff. I technically shouldn't even be talking to you. Not really. Is my accent too thick?"

Strawn shook his head. She looked younger than he was, and had high cheekbones and that nose that made him think of Helen of Troy. He wondered if Evanthia had seen Helen of Troy, if she'd even existed.

"Are you part of a university?"

Evanthia tapped her ear, uncomprehending.

"You said you were a scholar," Strawn said, suddenly uncertain. The steak and lobster tasted delicious.

"I am a scholar," Evanthia said. "Look, it's complicated, the relationship we have with the Consulate. Again, no grilling."

She took another big bite of her chop to emphasize the point. Strawn finished his own plate, not knowing what to say. He wanted to have sex with Evanthia, obviously.

"When does your shift end, Ms. Wayward?"

"Not a good idea, Mister Strawn," she said, shaking a fork at him. Was she a telepath, too?

"What's not a good idea?" he asked. Was he that obvious?

"Definitely frowned upon," Evanthia said. "Let's just be time-friends, okay?"

Strawn kicked himself for being so nakedly apparent, but what did he expect? She had over a thousand years on him, and time travelers were probably prepared to deal with any sort of situation.

"You can't fault a guy for thinking that," Strawn said. "You're beautiful."

"Thanks! It's all in the genes," Evanthia said, finishing her plate. "Man, was that ever prime. Do you want some dessert? Let's get some dessert."

"Have you been spying on me all this time?" Strawn asked. "This past month?"

Evanthia gave him an enigmatic smile. "Why? It's a big world, Mister Strawn. Why do you think I'd be focused solely on you? Even tiny East Thalerton is rife with sociological strata waiting to be mined. I could have a career in this place."

"Why? Because I was thinking about you," Strawn said. "The future, I mean. When you replied, I couldn't believe it."

"Did you decipher the note I sent?" Evanthia asked. "No, of course not."

"Decipher? It's a blank page."

Evanthia tapped her teeth with a long blue fingernail, then waved over a tray of desserts that she'd apparently already ordered. A piece of triple chocolate cake, almost black to the eye, and a cup of vanilla ice cream.

"There's blank and then there's blank," Evanthia said, taking a bite of the cake. "So good! I love doing live-in research; the food is just so funtastic."

"Fantastic," Strawn said. "That's the word."

"Really? How prongish of me! Funtastic makes so much more sense!"

Strawn watched her devour the cake, then wash it down with the ice cream. He got some coffee, while Evanthia polished off the ice cream.

"Whoops. My break's almost up," she said, glancing at her watch. Strawn felt disappointed. They hadn't talked about anything significant.

"Take me with you," he blurted out. Evanthia wiped her lips with a napkin.

"I can't do that," Evanthia said. "You know that."

Strawn wanted desperately to go with her. Anywhere. Anywhen. Evanthia got up and held out her slender hand.

"It was really prime to meet you, Mister Strawn," she said. "But if Annabella sees me culling time over here, I'm in for it."

"Killing time," Strawn said, desperate to keep her a moment or two longer.

"You can't kill time, Mister Strawn," Evanthia said, laughing. "But you can cull it, if you have the means. Whoops! Pretend I didn't just say that."

"When do you get off?" Strawn asked, taking her hand in his own sweaty palm. He didn't want to sound like he was pleading.

"Today's my last day," she said. "Then I'm gone. Way, way gone. A month or two back home, and then off to Thera."

"Please," Strawn said. "Please take me with you."

Evanthia's mossy eyes softened a bit, and she gave him a friend-hug. "I just can't do that, Mister Strawn. You know, rules and stuff. Thanks for the flowers, though. Totally prime."

She walked away, giving him a last look before scooping up her serving tray and disappearing behind the swinging doors, flowers in hand. She looked happy, not sad. She looked beautiful.

Strawn just stood there, gape-mouthed, left with the bill.

TIME'S UP

Strawn had rehearsed the encounter in his head, over and over again, wondering what he should have done. He hadn't known what to expect from the future. He cursed himself for not even taking a picture of her, though she didn't look too different from anybody else.

He had envisioned himself running through those swinging doors and grabbing Evanthia and kissing her, time-friendship notwithstanding. He saw himself managing to persuade Ms. Wayward to transport him to her time, so he could be the exchange student and learn about the future. He saw himself patenting the unusual paper and the envelope, making a fortune on it. He saw himself taking the sample of Evanthia's blood from the napkin and getting it genotyped, and perhaps patented as well. He saw himself setting fire to Fine Restaurant a month later, or putting out the fire and preventing it from burning down, just to spite her.

In a quantum sense, he'd already done all of those things. He realized that the pregnant possibilities of each moment lent themselves to an infinite array of combinations, and when one factored in not only everyone alive, but everyone who would be alive, and cut across time and space, the possibilities went beyond the infinite. At least to his brutish 21st Century mind.

And knowing that, Strawn wrote note after note, encapsulating it and burying it in his yard, begging, pleading, threatening, cursing, entreating, nagging, cajoling—everything he could think of, trying to get Evanthia to pay him another visit. But she never wrote back. Maybe that was how it was done in the future.

Fine Restaurant burned down, and Strawn clipped the article on it and put it in one of the capsules, trying to demonstrate that he was fit for the future, by being sane enough, pragmatic enough to let what would happen occur unimpeded, like those documentary filmmakers who watched impalas get eaten by hyenas.

Strawn looked at his back lot, aerated and overturned by his endless efforts, and wondered if Evanthia was even receiving them, or if anybody else in the Consulate was. Looking at his map (because he'd plotted out the area—it was like an archeological dig in reverse—he'd even sent his yard map in a note to Evanthia), he thought he had one more open area he could use.

He'd written a note to the Consulate, begging them to let him spend time in the future, but they never sent anybody else—at least nobody that he recognized. Part of him hoped that, as a temporally compromised individual (as Evanthia had called him), he might merit additional study. In fact, he was more than sure that they had somebody monitoring him, just to keep him from doing anything rash. But if a temporal agent was watching him, they never made their presence known, and so Strawn looked into cryogenics and the biomechanics of longevity, thinking that perhaps he could wait them out, frozen in a tube and ready to be defrosted and reanimated when the 31st Century rolled along. Then he'd have a word or two to say to Evanthia, and wouldn't she be surprised to see him!

But while the biomechanics of it all made sense to Strawn, the economics of it were far beyond him. Only tycoons and heirs were able to afford things like that, or reiterative cloning. Strawn didn't have the money for it, and so he was forced to come to terms with being stuck in 2011, and doomed to die in the meaty part of the 21st Century, after all.

After that, he devoted his free time to deciphering the blank page she'd sent, wondering if she had been joking with him, or if there really was a message locked within the seemingly empty page. But he couldn't break the code, if there was even a code to break. He just didn't know.

It was a bitter thing, being a man of the future, stuck in the here and now. He thought that as he watched the spikey teens beating parking meters with triluminum bats and heard the crackle of aerocopters as they knifed their way over crumbling East Thalerton, spotlights glaring and speakers blaring. Walking back to his little place, feeling smaller than ever before, and without even the solace of hope to comfort him, Strawn tried to turn his attention to where he was, and to forget about Evanthia entirely.

He reset the future Chronometer, the one she had sent back to him, and kept it on his desk, watching it tick off time as he went through the rest of his life. He did that until he died of thyroid cancer.

000,000,013YEAR:115DAY:05HOUR:08MIN:56SEC

Per his will, the Chronometer and the blank page were buried with him, and the Chronometer kept ticking for a very long time.

He hadn't told anybody.

Mission Control

NEHRU HANNIGAN knew when he was wanted; as a Mediator, it was his business to know. The Mediation Department's involvement in the Renco Mars Mission became inevitable when Harrod Simco, the Mission Director, showed him the video feed of the Martian Astropreneurs at the Phase 1 base. Connor "Kip" Haversham was fighting with Erich Lengel, the former holding a hefty wrench, the latter trying to baste Haversham with a blowtorch.

"It's not my fault," Haversham yelled, his voice crackling on the monitor. At this distance, the feed was a bit spotty, the lag was punitive. Lengel, younger and all lean muscle, turned that torch toward Haversham, ever closer, until the older Astropreneur, the Mission Commander, flipped Lengel and knocked him out with a blow of the wrench. The crunch wasn't terminal; Lengel was still breathing while Haversham scrambled across the floor to catch the rolling torch before it seared the VacuSealed walls of the compound.

"Control!" Haversham yelled into the camera. "The food isn't here!!"

Simco stopped the recording with a swipe of his hand.

"This wasn't going out live, was it?" Hannigan asked. Simco shook his head. The delay alone prevented anything like that from happening. The two men couldn't have looked more different, with Simco tanned like beef jerky, silver eye lenses offering UV protection and a deadly stare, while his hair, surely implanted, was thick and lustrous black. For a man of 79, Simco looked stunningly, unapologetically fit in his blue suit accented with a fat, coral-colored tie.

Nehru was about half Simco's age, softer, caramel-colored and fond of tan, chocolate, and ivory hues in his clothing, with an ivory turtleneck and a thick gold pinky ring set with a ruby the size of a cat's eye. Hannigan chalked up his buttery complexion to gene therapy.

"We're in a jam," Simco said. "Everything depends on that Mars mission succeeding, and we've got those Astropreneurs up there without any damned food."

"What happened?"

"Equipment failure," Simco said. "Rocket made reentry well enough, payload deployed its ass right into the landscape—pulverized. Nothing but splinters left. Not wood, either—titanium. No food."

Hannigan nodded knowingly, because he knew that corporate clients liked knowing nods. He'd read the files that Simco had provided, but he wanted to hear it from the Man himself.

Renco had planned for a multistage Mars mining operation that would allow a permanent human presence on the red planet. Several rockets had been launched at Mars, each with a different part of the larger colonization project as its payload. First went drones and building materials. The drones were then remote-employed to build the compound, at low cost.

Twenty-six interlocking compounds had been built: Sections A through Z, in an interlocking webwork of polysteel and Kevlar. After the drones had built the Mars base, the second rocket arrived, containing robots and hardware like atmosphere generators and other life support systems, including water reclamation, power plants, and air purification. The robots dutifully set these things up, with humans lending a hand via the drones.

The on-site robots included a Takoro G-11 Surveyor, a Mikihama "Jobbot" Multipurpose Labor Unit, a Jendalanna

Medical Robot, and an Erotix Lambda Lovebot (because the male-to-female ratio on the colony was 7 to 1). The robots all went online without incident, the Jobbot working under the guidance of the Takoro to get things running smoothly, including firing the reactors, water acquisition and purification, climate control, and general troubleshooting.

After that, food stores arrived at the colony. These had been carefully selected to represent three years' worth of nutritionally balanced meals for the 14 Astropreneurs that had accepted jobs with the Renco Mars Project, a contracted operation that gave them each (pending survival) a considerable stake in Phase 2 of the Renco Mars Outpost and a back salary of 38 million TransYen that would be redeemable upon return.

One slight snag was that the G-11 Surveyor had proven unable to locate the food stores before the Renco 1 made its spectacular landing on May 17.

Renco had subcontracted with Ellipses International, which had, in turn, subcontracted to Melovex Ltd., to find the appropriate personalities that would staff Renco 1, the first commercial ship to Mars. The crew had been carefully selected from over 10,000 applicants, 500 semifinalists, and after 50 finalists had been chosen, it was whittled down to the 14 Astropreneurs who showed the proper balance of ethnicity and pluck (to say nothing of photogenicity, for Renco had crafted a show around the mission, and all of the Astropreneurs were good-looking, or at least interestingly ugly).

While the heavily male-oriented audience would seem to have mandated a heavier female crew load, Risk Assessment determined that the likelihood of the Phase 1 team surviving intact until initiation of Phase 2 was about 40%—at least six Astropreneurs were expected to die, and the Renco analysts thought it would be a ratings disaster to have beautiful women killed on Mars. The smaller number of women would increase their value, and also allow for some pert confrontations with the Lovebot, who was expected to be the dark horse for the men's affections.

Advertising revenue from the Phase 1 mission would be poured into financing the Phase 2 project, and executives at Renco were anticipating a huge audience share for the overall campaign, and put considerable money into hyping the event as it proceeded.

To date, eight Astropreneurs had died as a result of the food crisis. Riots. Hoarding. Panic. Hysteria. It was Day 39 of the Mission.

"No relief ship can possibly make it in time, can it?" Hannigan asked.

"One year, at the very earliest," Simco said. "Using the best rockets we have. A very expensive little operation."

Simco had a monitor wall, showing all aspects of the Mars Mission being recorded. Some images were stills, while others seemed to be live feeds.

"Why haven't you scrubbed the mission?" Hannigan said.

"They won't make it back," Simco said. "We're talking starvation, here."

"What about the lunar base?" Hannigan asked.

"No good," Simco said. "Too far away. This is a disaster we've got, Nehru. We wouldn't have brought in Mediators if it wasn't."

Hannigan nodded. It certainly did feel disastrous to him, but at Mediation, they were used to disasters. It was their specialty.

The Mars lander had enough food for 90 days with a full crew load, 180 days with seven crew, and 270 days with three. They could probably double the amount of days if they rationed the food stores from the outset.

The G-11 Surveyor failed to reconcile the telemetry findings of Mission Control, which put them in the shadow of the Olympus Mons. This fueled speculation that the G-11 had been damaged on reentry, and prompted Mission Control to run exhaustive diagnostics on the Surveyor, turning up no apparent error in the robot. The G-11s were known for their durability and reliability in the field, and Takoro's spokesperson assured Renco that no G-11 had failed in its mission, including far more dangerous stints in asteroid mining and comet surveying.

"Original crew…staff commitment was 14, right?" Nehru asked, already knowing the answer. "That means only six staff remain. That should almost double the lander's food supply duration. Longer, if the staff eat the bodies of the others. And if you immediately launch a fast relief ship to the base."

Simco shook his head again. "We've run simulations on this. No relief any sooner than a year's time, using every available resource."

"What about competitors?" Nehru asked. "Anybody else in the region? Asteroid miners?"

"They're not equipped for a rescue like that," Simco said. "Chthonix relies mostly on drones; they're crew-minimized. Symworld Transindustrial is in the midst of fiery labor negotiations. And Allstaroid has pulled its fleets, also pending labor disputes."

Hannigan knew what Simco wanted, but he wanted Simco to ask him. It was part of the dance, and Nehru wasn't about to lead.

"What about lifeboats?" Nehru asked.

Simco nodded. "Three shuttles. But one of them is inoperative."

"Any food on those?"

"Emergency rations. That still just buys them, at most, six months," Simco said. "Look, we have to broadcast something. We've had killer ratings around this story, and we can't just let it, you know, die. I can't broadcast those poor bastards starving up there."

"Have they run a distress beacon?" Nehru asked.

"Standard procedure. But we're the first out there. Nobody's close. We made a point of getting there ahead of the competition. Cinnabar Ltd. isn't due there for two years."

Nehru saw one of the crewmen screwing the Lambda Lovebot. "Who's that?"

Simco looked. "That would be Lang. The prevert."

"A pervert, eh?" Hannigan asked. Simco nodded.

"He's underwent total preversion as soon as the food problem was revealed," Simco said. "He's in love with Trixie."

"Trixie?"

"That's what they call the Lovebot," Simco said. It turned out that Crewman Lang had become emotionally attached to the Lovebot, and had become possessive of it. Since each staff member contracted to have equal access to Trixie, Lang's usurpation and subsequent abduction of the Lovebot led to an increasingly tense confrontation between him and the other crew, and with crewman Don Alutto, who never liked Lang to begin with.

Nehru had watched the segment when it had been broadcast, edited in the clipped style that Renco preferred, emphasizing dynamism.

"Mars needs women!" Lang said with a laugh, taking a hit from a cigarette, sitting in the Martian Lounge in Section M. "But, you know, sometimes you just have to take matters into your own hands."

"I look forward to getting to know the crew a lot better," Trixie purred, looking well-lubed and pristinely chromed. "I find people to be endlessly surprising."

Erotix didn't even bother to simulate flesh. They opted for a cool, metallic sleekness in their Lambda line, emphasizing robust performance and durability.

"Lang's a crazy son of a bitch," Alutto said to the camera, looking haggard, his beard a week old on his lantern jaw. "He talks to the thing. I mean, Trixie's just a machine, you know? He's been off his nut ever since we landed and found out there wasn't any food."

"He doesn't appreciate her," Lang said to the camera. "Trixie's sensitive. She understands me. Don treats her bad."

Trixie had been programmed to meet the sexual needs of every staff member, including a truncated pillow talk sequence and biographical database that allowed for the unit to service each crewperson according to their particular preferences. Erotix, Inc. was proud to feature its Lovebot on the

Renco Mars Mission, and was glad to see Trixie perform so well.

"Wanking in here all day with Trixie," Alutto bellowed, hitting Trixie with a pipe. "We're [bleep]ing starving here, mate!"

"You killed her!" Lang screamed, getting into a fight with Alutto.

"Please don't be mad, Don," Trixie said, touching her broken cranial carapace. Alutto had been locked up after that, as Erotix's people were howling at the damage to their flagship Lambda unit.

"I remain fully functional, despite some cosmetic flaws," Trixie said. But nobody else would have anything to do with her. She was damaged goods.

Nehru scratched his chin a bit. "We could just run Lang with Trixie. Go full porno until we can think of something else."

Simco shrugged. "We ran it for a week after the Alutto thing. Plenty of fuck machines at home. Lambda Unit sales are up, but we lost some audience share. Look, Hanny, we need you."

Just like that, Hannigan snapped the trap on Simco. "How much?"

"15 million TransYen," Simco said. "Full Mediation on this."

"Not enough," Hannigan said. "40 million. And I want points and shares on the Phase 2 mission."

"There's not going to be a Phase 2," Simco grumbled. "Not at the rate we're going. We've basically handed Mars to Cinnabar."

"I will deliver you Phase 2 on a platter," Hannigan said. "But I want shares. A lot. We'll have people begging to go to Mars."

Nehru was supremely confident in his ability as a Mediator. He knew that only Mediation could possibly save the Phase 1 mission. With only a few staff alive on the base, it would be a breeze.

First, Nehru gave the go-ahead to his action teams, which consisted of Kino Gossett, who was in charge of Simulation, Nalia Shore, who was in charge of Scripting, Bedford Rockwell, who was in charge of Public Relations, and Callista Forbes, who handled Audience Analysis.

He met with them at the Renco High Security Antarctica Section, where they watched waves break upon the green plantation shores. Callista was his brightest star, with an amphetamine-scrubbed brain that crunched numbers like a machine. Callista was pale as milk but with a heart that was oily black, and Nehru had assumed she would be his successor, once he moved on to bigger things. She kept manicured fingers on the audience pulse, running and coordinating focus groups and real-time audience reactions to the story. If anybody so much as sneezed at the Phase 1 Outpost, Callista knew which audience members got colds.

Kino had already run sim demos of the Astropreneurs, a project Nehru had set for him when he first got an inkling of trouble on Mars. He had run video footage and scanned samples of all of the Renco Mars staff, and began running them through simulated actions, using computers to build a database of voice samples that would offer a credible impression of the crew.

As Kino and his 10-member team sweated on that, Nalia had her freelancers work on storylines to weave into the existing narrative currently in place on Mars. Again, this was spec work, dependent on Nehru being able to get Simco to sign over the project to him, but Nalia's team began writing several parallel narratives that could be stitched into the existing story without undue difficulty. She assured Nehru that it would be doable.

While this was going on, Bedford began leaking stories to the media about trouble at the Mars base. This was intended to draw some more fire toward Renco, which would allow more pressure to be put on Simco to seek a solution, which Nehru was only too happy to provide. A young, college-educated member of the Free Theocratic Party, Bedford's all-American good looks and southern hemispheric charm played well with the hacks he dealt with.

Nehru would focus strictly on Mediation, and, of course, oversight.

"We have six stranded Mars colonists," he said. "And no means of rescuing them. Renco's offered us a generous contract to get them out of this situation, so that's what we're going to do. I want reports from you all before proceeding. Callista, we'll start with you."

Callista nodded, crossing her long legs and leaning forward with a hologram display unit, which flashed to life, showing bar graphs and some bullet-pointed lists.

"Audiences identify most with Kip Haversham and Aida L'Puissant," she said. "The two of them together give us almost 70% of the target audience demographic. We should sculpt any narrative around those two. Perhaps a desperate love interest or something. Like doomed lovers."

Nalia raised her hand in disagreement.

"I don't think the word 'doom' should go anywhere near this project," she said. "We want the audiences to leave this one on a positive note, a sense of hope and promise."

"A happy ending," Kino said with a groan. "How're we going to explain when nobody turns up?"

"You'll have them turn up," Nehru said. "That's the whole point of this operation, isn't it? We can hire doubles, if we need to. The audience has seen some of the Astropreneurs die. They're highly motivated to see the remaining six survive. So, that's what we'll give them. And by 'we' I mean 'you,' of course."

Kino sighed atop his earlier groan. Bedford chimed in. "I don't see any reason why we can't make people believe that things turned out okay up there. We can work with Nalia to put together some human interest stories—like 'Where are they now?' and that kind of thing. So what if people can't track them down? What we can't perfectly match, we can simulate, and what we can't simulate, we can mediate. People never look the same on video as they do in person—we can have actors fill the roles. With the appropriate nondisclosure forms we can do whatever we want, and with the money that was going to go to the Astropreneurs freed up, we can use that to pay the actors."

Nehru took a glance at the status screen. It looked like the Astropreneurs had factionalized, with three barricading themselves in one of the main storage wings, while the others ransacked the base for other resources.

"Not a bad idea," Hannigan said. "Though actors are talky, and are likely to get the word out to the newspress that doubles had been hired to portray the Astropreneurs."

Callista spoke up.

"I would think that audiences would be inclined to believe anything they're told, including multiple competing storylines. What if we market-tested several of them? Say, Storyline A: the Astropreneurs successfully established Outpost 1, overcoming all odds—High Inspirational; Storyline B: the Astropreneurs died heroic deaths on Mars—Aspirational Sacrifice; Storyline C: the Astropreneurs were forced (through circumstances beyond their control) to abandon Outpost 1 and return to Earth—Bittersweet Triumph; Storyline D: a plague broke out at the Mars base, requiring indefinite quarantine of the Astropreneurs—Technological Terror; Storyline E: the Astropreneurs disappeared, perhaps as a result of alien abduction—Enigmatic Mystery; Storyline F: Asteroid/Meteorite/Comet destroys station—Act of God™. There's any number of scenarios we could try out."

Nalia hunched over her holopad, busy jotting down what Callista had said, though it was clear from her expression that she did not relish having to craft six different storylines for the sake of Audience Analysis. Her sidelong glance to Nehru confirmed this.

"We scrubbed Storyline F," Callista said, "Because every amateur and professional astronomer would be busy trying to find which chunk of space debris did in the station. There's a high crank factor we could exploit on this, pitting our word against those of disputants, but all it would take would be somebody to look at the surface and see no sign of a crater, and we'd be screwed."

"We could nuke the base," Nehru said. "Would that leave a crater?"

"Sure," Callista said. "But again there are detection issues. It's too flashy."

"Okay, so we scrub that last one," Nehru said.

Bedford liked Callista's ideas. "People are already skeptical of everything they see, even as they are more credulous than ever. I don't see why we shouldn't audience-test those scenarios, see which plays the best. Then we can build the whole campaign around it, leverage it for the end zone. There's no point in running a scenario that the audience won't like. That'll just hurt the client."

Again, Nehru's eyes flicked to the monitor screens, in hope of finding inspiration there. Lang was still with Trixie, while Aida L'Puissant and Kip Haversham were hunkered down in their secured section of Outpost 1, amid boxes of food. They looked tired, though still well-fed.

Hannigan tuned out his team and turned up the volume on them. Aida looked especially lovely, like a bronzed Amazon, with hair elaborately braided. They'd cast her well.

"We're going to die, aren't we?" she said to Haversham, who was taping the handle of a pipe wrench, testing its swing.

"Yeah," he said. "Sutter and Korth have the shuttle wing. No idea about Blaine, and we know where Lang is. Those shuttles can't take us anywhere. Well, they could take you and me, but not all six of us."

Aida's face was hard. "I don't want to die."

"Nobody does," Kip said, giving the wrench another swing.

"You think the two of us could make it?" she asked.

"We've got the food, don't we?" he said, giving one of the supply boxes a swat. "We might have enough to take one more person."

Aida appeared to be doing calculations in her head. "But who?"

"Blaine," Haversham said. "If she's still alive. Sutter and Korth aren't worth spit to me. Not after what they've done."

"What about him?" Aida asked, pointing toward Lengel, who was still laying on the ground.

"Lengel's dead," Haversham said.

"What? I thought I saw—"

"Dead, I said."

Nehru watched the autocam move in tight on Aida's face, capturing her eyes. Conspirator's eyes, hard, like little shiny beads of moldavium.

"What, then?"

"We take the Shuttle Bay," Haversham said. "Pack the food and we leave."

"Murder?"

"Self-defense," Haversham said. "It's either that or we sit and slowly starve to death."

"What about Lang?" she asked.

Haversham shook his head. Nehru's eyes flicked to Lang's quarters, where he was being sexually abused by Trixie, per his consent. Steel fingers closed around his neck as he came. From where Nehru sat, it looked like Lang had taken advantage of the damage to Trixie's carapace to do some on-the-spot modifications to her program, the wires and fiber optic lines dangling from her head like tangled hair. Hannigan hadn't thought Lang had it in him, but Erotix's ad campaigns did tout the user-friendliness of the Lambda Line.

"Dance for me, Jeffrey," Trixie whispered, straddling him, while he spasmed into unconsciousness, the Lovebot fucking him to death, over and over again.

"Can't go with that," Nehru mumbled, looking at another screen. He saw Sutter, Korth, and Blaine, looking lean and hungry. Korth had a pipe, while Sutter had a torch. Heather Blaine just looked scared.

"We can hold three," Sutter said. "You want aboard, you play ball with us, Blaine."

"Fine," she said. Sutter and Korth were miners, not pilots. Hulking and broad-shouldered, they could easily overpower

Haversham and L'Puissant, without even factoring Blaine into it. However, they couldn't fly the shuttle, which meant that Haversham had to survive, at least until they were launched.

Nehru watched them plot. Sutter and Korth had been chosen for their ability to work, not because they were telegenic. Dark-hued and heavy-browed, they had been a sullen presence onscreen. Compared with the lithe Blaine, it was Beauty and the Beasts.

"Storyline G: Beauty and the Beasts," Nehru said. "Lovely woman at the mercy of two hulking half-men; Storyline C: The Doomed Lovers, Haversham and L'Puissant, in their desperate bid for escape."

Callista sighed.

"What?" Bedford asked. "What about the others?"

"What's the turnaround on these broadcasts?" Nehru asked.

"11 minutes." from Callista.

"We've got two factions, people," Nehru said. "The Beasts in the Shuttle Bay, and Haversham and L'Puissant. Who do we operationalize as Renco's spokespeople?"

The team thought it over for a bit, while Sutter and Korth crept their way toward the warehouse area. Blaine was locked in a storage unit within the Shuttle Bay.

"Do we want those brutes to represent our client?" Hannigan asked. Bedford shook his head, while Callista wrinkled her nose in distaste. Nalia shrugged, jotting things onto her holopad.

"Blaine's pretty," Kino said. "Pretty is good."

"Right," Nehru said. "Pretty is good. Let's go with pretty."

Hannigan tapped his handphone and put a call into Operations, who was responsible for the drones. "Have the drones deployed around the perimeter holding L'Puissant and Haversham. Sutter and Korth are making a move on them. Have the drones seal them off. Yes, Simco's signed off on this."

"Three crew can survive a year," Nehru said. "Looks like Lang blew his wad with Trixie and Lengel's dead. That leaves Sutter and Korth. We drop them from the show and the food problem is solved. We scrub the mission and send them to Luna. They return as heroes."

"That's a lot of show to fill," Nalia said. "Why'd they have to leave?"

"You'll come up with something," Nehru said.

Nehru noted the movement of the drones into position with satisfaction. Kino looked at the monitor wall.

"What are those, T36 labor drones?"

"I don't know."

They had arms and an array of tools. Tools could just as easily be weapons. Nehru tapped another button on his phone.

"I want to talk to Haversham," he said. In a tense 11 minutes, he was linked to the warehouse, Haversham gazing into an autocam. "Kip, I'm here to help you out of your situation. As it stands, your colony is going to starve to death. You know this. Sutter and Korth are making their way to your bunker to try to get you. They want off Mars as badly as you do. Now, we don't want those two goons clogging the airwaves. It's going to be difficult enough mediating this thing as it stands. What I need from you is your agreement that you'll not breathe a word of this to anybody outside. For that, we'll help you get off-planet and back home, safe."

Nehru and the others waited while the message went out.

"Anybody been to Luna?" he asked.

Callista nodded. "It's pretty. The Hotel Intergalactic is great."

"Nice accommodations?"

"Out of this world," Callista said. "Like their ads say."

Nehru winked at her. "I don't trust advertising."

"Smart man," Callista said, prompting Nalia to roll her eyes. They waited while the signal from Mars returned, the endless delay.

Haversham's face was sweaty. "We all can't leave. The shuttle won't take that many."

"I know," Nehru said. "There's room for you and Aida. Maybe Blaine, too. That's it."

And again, they waited.

"Where is Blaine?" he asked.

"She's with Sutter and Korth," Nehru said. "Sort of. They've got her tied up in the Shuttle Bay, but she's with them, against you and Aida."

Nehru scratched an itch behind one of his hands. "It's really distracting, talking like this. Hard to keep focused."

"Think about them," Nalia said. "The pressure they're under."

"Sure, sure," Nehru said. "Hotel Intergalactic. Is that four stars?"

"Five," Callista said.

"Five stars," Nehru said. "I can't believe they'd be able to get that kind of ranking way out there."

"It's the only hotel of its type," Callista said. "The view is unbelievable."

"Yeah, but five stars," Nehru said. "I don't buy it."

"You're too skeptical for your own good," Callista said. The signal returned.

Haversham bit his lip, cursing under his breath. Because of the good sound work, Nehru heard every word of it. He glanced at Sutter and Korth, working their way through the compounds, discussing what they would do. Korth wanted to take Aida and leave Blaine, while Sutter preferred Blaine. They bickered about it as they went.

"Aida and I want off," Haversham said.

"Fine," Nehru said. "Hold on."

He toggled a button on his phone, putting him in touch with Operations. "Have the drones lie in wait for Sutter and Korth. Let them get to the doors, and then cut them off. Have the drones seal off the doors and let the G-11 go after the crewmen. You can override the robots, correct? Well, get the authorization codes, and fast."

He clicked back.

"So, is this an oral contract?" Nehru asked. And again, they waited. "What were you doing up on Luna, Cal?"

"Business," she said. "The Evernaut account."

"Ah, yes," Nehru said. "Evernaut. Man, what a mess that was."

"It wasn't that bad," Nalia said. "I liked the Evernauts."

Nehru shrugged. The signal came back.

Haversham was nodding. Apparently, Aida could hear it as well.

"We're not waiving our agreed-upon fees," Haversham said. "We got way more than we bargained for on this one."

"Sure, sure," Nehru said. "Hold on, Kip."

He didn't want the drone pilots doing any of the dirty work, because that would be murder. Not that anybody would know. But the pilots would know, and Nehru didn't want them feeling guilty about it.

"What about Blaine?" Aida asked. "We can't honestly leave her."

"She's with them," Haversham said. "Let her stay with them."

Nehru liked the sound of that. Some iron in the mix. He knew he'd picked correctly when he'd settled on Haversham and L'Puissant.

"We're going to clear a way for you," Nehru said, motioning for another phone. Callista beat the others to it, giving him her phone. He jotted a number down and handed it to her. She dialed, then he held out his hand, putting that phone to his other ear.

"Mission Control," it said.

"I need an override on Door 127. It's locked on-site," Nehru said.

"Who is this?"

"Hannigan," he said. The silence on the other side of the line was itself a reward.

"Done," the voice said.

"And the override commands on the G-11? How about the Jobbot?"

"We have them," the voice said.

"Great," Hannigan said. "Have them go after Sutter and Korth."

"Excuse me?"

"You heard me," he said. "I'll take full responsibility."

"You'd better," the voice said.

"Fine, fine," Nehru said, watching Sutter and Korth get attacked by the G-11, aided by the Jobbot, who pinned the men to the wall with its massive arms while the G-11 drove surveyor stakes through their skulls with a pneumatic chuff that made the camera image flicker a moment. The men twitched a bit, tacked to the VacuSealed walls by their heads.

On another monitor, Aida looked in that direction. "Did you hear that, Kip? Like a thump?"

Haversham didn't respond, kept his eyes on the autocam. Blue eyes. Astronaut eyes.

"They're coming for us," he muttered.

"Who?"

"Sutter and Korth," he said. Nehru clicked back on.

"Door 127 is open, Kip," Nehru said. "Follow the trail of doors to the Shuttle Bay. We're cutting off Sutter and Korth, got them pinned down in J Section."

Nehru glanced at the monitors. Both men had stopped twitching, while the G-11 circled the room, arms flailing.

"What about the food?" Kip asked.

"We'll have the Jobbot deliver it," Nehru said. "For now, get the shuttle up and running."

Kip and Aida exchanged a worried look and crept out of the warehouse, working their way to the Shuttle Bay. Callista looked at Nehru with undisguised admiration.

Nehru had Mission Control and Operations run the Jobbot and the drones to the Shuttle Bay, transporting the food there, while Haversham and L'Puissant confronted Blaine, who was gratefully terrified to see them.

"Your pals are locked up in J Section," Haversham said.

"Pals? I'm not with them, Kip." Blaine replied.

"Look, I know. *They* know," Haversham said. "Renco's getting us out of here."

Not entirely true, but the Astropreneur only had limited information. Mediation was its own entity, affiliated with Renco, but on a client basis, not a subsidiary. It made the job easier.

"We're saved!" Blaine said, but Haversham was dour.

"Aida and I are," he said. "You and your pals need to work out another deal."

Nehru didn't object to Blaine coming along. An unstable triad was better than a stable dyad, as far as he was concerned.

"It's okay," Nehru said. "Blaine can come."

The Jobbot and the drones hauled in the food from the warehouse while the Astropreneurs readied the shuttle. Blaine was wondering about Lang and Sutter and Korth, but Nehru told her a relief ship was being rerouted to them. Not enough supplies to handle all six of them, but enough to rescue the others later.

The eight confirmed dead Astropreneurs were freeze-dried in Section H. Nehru had the drones haul Sutter and Korth there, and Trixie was pried off Lang, so that he, too, could be deposited there. This occurred without the Astropreneurs' knowing it, as Nehru figured they had been through enough stress as it was, and their ignorance would give them authenticity.

Hannigan's team took notes while this was going on, each working on their respective areas, crafting the appropriate narrative and visuals that would convey the needed feelings with regard to Renco Phase 1 Mars Mission.

Nehru was already thinking ahead to the Phase 2 Mission, wondering what would come of it, and how it would play with the Phase 1 Mission, assuming the next wave of Astropreneurs reached the Outpost. He thought perhaps they could simply shut down the base when the time had come, and let the drones disassemble it, and let the Martian windstorms scour the area clean.

The shuttle was loaded, and the Astropreneurs buckled themselves in, bound for Luna. With only three survivors from the mission, Nehru calculated a savings of 114 million TransYen for Renco, in terms of contract wages. There were no payouts for families of the deceased, since Renco had specifically wanted unattached singles for the Phase 1 project. Phase 2 or 3 would allow for marrieds, and, eventually, the first Martian childbirth, for which there would be a great deal of publicity.

Nehru watched the Astropreneurs blast free of Mars's limp gravity and leave behind the horrors of the Phase 1 Outpost.

As they flew, Nehru beamed them nondisclosure forms (they had signed ones before joining the mission, but these were additional ones that covered the irregularities that had occurred at the Outpost). All three of them readily signed, and Nehru was pleased to present that to Simco, who signed off on it.

Nehru had bought four weeks' time by broadcasting reruns of the Mars mission, including a two-hour introductory special that featured the Astropreneurs and ran biographical pre-recorded segments of them, including some memorials for the known dead.

Astropreneur Deke Auckerman accidentally breached the inner wall of Section W while testing some of the mine equipment, and was sucked through the hole he'd made in the VacuSealed wall, becoming the first fatality, freeze-dried on the Martian surface. Auckerman's death was, however, effectively audience-transitioned through the work of News Analyst Corrie Retsina, who praised the heroism and risk-taking of the Astropreneurs, and ran a memorial biography of Auckerman that made no mention of his drinking problem. All of the Astropreneurs had agreed to record these pre-mortem spots.

"I've always wanted to be a spaceman," Deke said to the camera, emphatically, fading into a slow-motion shot of him walking away, gazing at the stars above.

Engineer Mandolin Russo, along with the Jobbot, went on a thrilling operation to patch the exterior wall of the compound Deke had ruptured. This was deemed a mission narrowly focused enough not to require heavy editing by Mediation, and with the time delay between signal and broadcast, editors were able to ensure no reference to the food problem turned up in the broadcast, and the audience ate it up.

"Nobody said space was safe," Deke said. "I don't remember that being said anywhere, but it's a risk I'm willing to take."

//

Preston Walker, director of Renco Mission Control, complained to Simco about Hannigan's use of the G-11 to murder Crewmen Sutter and Korth.

"System malfunction," Simco said. "Happens all the time. That's the narrative we're using with that, if we have to. Nobody killed them; it was the G-11 that did it."

"Takoro's not going to be happy to know that their product was misused in that fashion," Walker said. He was a young man, nearly the age of Simco's only son, Destin.

"You let me worry about Takoro," Simco said. "Not your problem."

"Hannigan," Walker said, watching the sim-Astropreneurs enjoying their Thanksgiving feast on the monitors, after having recovered the food canisters after all, in a daring cross-country ride in land rovers, after Kip Haversham had successfully mapped out the actual location of the food stores, which had been blown off-course by the howling Martian winds.

"Our ratings are huge, Pres," Simco said. "Hannigan's people are scripting this for the next three years, until we've got Phase 2 online and can get that rolling."

Walker was not pleased. He knew he'd never command another Martian mission again, after the food debacle. It had been a design flaw of the parachutes. It had been rectified, and would be put to use on Phase 2, but Walker would not command it.

"Space," Kip Haversham said. "Who can resist it?"

Walker attempted to blow the whistle on the Phase 1 cover-up, but Bedford Rockwell had let it be known (in a round-about way) that Preston Walker was a habitual amphetamine abuser, and that paranoia was a known side effect of amphetamine abuse. When several hundred grams of amphetamine had been found at his property in White Lake, it was a done deal. Renco's Psychological Affairs Department had Walker institutionalized for his own self-protection. Sadly, Walker hanged himself a month after being admitted. No one knows who smuggled the necktie in.

"I hear it snows dry ice," Aida L'Puissant said. "I'd like to see that just once."

The sim-Astropreneurs continued to work and thrive on the Mars Outpost, with Nalia's team running several story-lines and subplots that were woven around individual crew, based on Callista's projections.

"More women crewmen—crewpeople. Staff," Jeff Lang said. "You know what I mean."

Gradually, as part of the grand strategy, a series wrap-up was planned. This would wean audiences away from Phase 1 and get them ready for Phase 2.

"We're all gonna die," Mandolin Russo said, laughing. "I mean, everybody dies. Well, almost everybody. Robots don't die, I guess."

Callista's demographic research showed that audiences were most intrigued by the presence of the robots on the Mars Outpost, and wanted more stories involving interactions between crew and robots. Renco worked out deals with the top manufacturers, offering brand-name exposure for their top models on Phase 2.

"I look forward to stimulating relationships with my fellow crew," Trixie said (pre-recorded).

Some groups said that a human presence on Mars was redundant, given the exemplary performance of the G-11 Surveyor and the Jobbot, as well as the piloted drones. There was no need for food, no need to worry about radiation poisoning (sadly, an unexpected hull breach killed 10 of the sim-crewmen in the second season; a micrometeorite was blamed). The episode was run around the clock, which dovetailed nicely with the evacuation of the Outpost by surviving Astropreneurs Haversham, L'Puissant, and Blaine.

Season Three was devoted to the shuttle's flight to Luna, with several episodes devoted to the departed crew.

The three survivors married on Luna Prime, and were interviewed on their honeymoon, all of them doing very well, their live interview with Lezzie Jrindakar garnering a commanding slice of the viewing audience.

"We're just happy to be alive," Kip said, beaming. "I'm the luckiest guy in the world."

"Which world?" Lezzie asked, prompting laughter. Aida got serious.

"We're really going to miss our fellow Astropreneurs," she said. "They were the best."

Blaine broke down and cried, but Nehru had his broadcast people edit that out of the live broadcast, which, thanks to the natural lunar delay cycle, allowed a cross-cut showing Blaine looking on, big-eyed and smiling, nodding at the others, instead.

Hannigan's excellent work got him the exclusive Mediation contract for the Phase 2 mission, as well as Mission Control Directorship. He promised even more excitement for that mission, and solemnly declared there would be far fewer fatalities during Phase 2.

He personally guaranteed it.

The Wordspeak Level-Set

1

PRISMACORE'S morning standup meeting went as Keene had expected it would go. Harrison Reid had arrived on time via zeppelin, looking corporate trim in lustrous pinstripes from bespoke suits from Singapore. His skin had attained a bronze hue from his weeks in the Pacific, shoring up the accounts with Beijing.

"What do you want to bet he's retiring?" Madison Milton asked in Keene's ear.

"Lunch," Keene said. "I'll bet you lunch that he is not."

They stood together at the glass-housed executive suite, the airships slicing the Chicago skyline in slow motion in the middle distance.

Madison worked with Keene in Acquisitions, and she looked polished as ever—burgundy manicured fingernails and a grey flannel suit and skirt and kitten heels of patent leather oxblood. She had her hair immaculately lacquered in a kind of wave of blonde that spilled into breakwater bangs over her chiseled face. She had a straight nose and big, brown eyes and a small mouth with prissy-kissy lips.

The other execs flocked around Reid, who held up his tanned hands as if he were a prophet of profit, a 650,000-yuan tourbillon movement Agafleuria platinum watch glittering at his wrist, and prepared to speak.

"Aces in their places," Reid said. "As part of the wordspeak level-set, line of sight, we're needing to be locked and loaded across all decisioning pathways from the get-go. We're seeking a full knowledge transfer, here. We're getting into bed with Beijing and we've got no room for zerotasking, am I clear?"

Keene glanced at the other executives, who nodded earnestly. Even Madison did.

"Wait," Keene said, whispering to Madison. "What did he just say?"

"Fully baked," Reid said. "On the cheap and fully operationalized, we're countering a yield loss that's a Prismacore win-win net-net."

The other executives applauded, and Keene followed suit.

"I want a fact pattern established in the face of the headwinds from Beijing," Reid said, glancing at Keene and freezing his blood. "Keene, you get to eat the frog, here—you unbundle the ghost work deliverables with Milton, get everything fully decisioned and gisted, full stop."

All of the eyes were on Keene and Milton, and Keene spoke up quickly.

"We're on it, Harrison," Keene said. "Absolutely."

"I'm already compiling a list of action items," Madison said, glancing at Keene. "I'm fully leveraging the legacied deliverables."

"Outstanding," Reid said. "Hammer out the details; I want to hit the perfect cadence on the languaging of our wallet share on this while you're busy weighing the pig."

Keene could feel himself sweating, the eyes on him, the hostile eyes, envious at the attention. Fat, pinstriped Gunderton from Compliance. Bespectacled, balding Mills from Accounting. Dour Windour from Brand. Different departments, but everyday adversaries.

Gunderton was quick to speak up, drawing Reid's eyes away from Keene and Milton. "Let's have a washup with the major players, Harrison."

"HR, we'll navigate around the pain points on this and squeeze the juice we need before we jump the couch," Madison said.

"Terrific," Reid said.

Keene looked from Madison to the others, and she winked at him, while Reid continued to unpack his presentation.

2

Keene cornered Madison in their open floor smartdesk, which Keene had managed to secure from Mills by the strategic use of elbows and quick-booking it *sotto voce* via his drone phone, which he'd pulled the moment they'd gotten out of the standing meeting with Reid.

"ANGELICA, book me Room 4659 ASAP," Keene said, while the other suits were barking orders into their own brillphones, as they were known. Smarter than smart, they were brill.

"On it, Keene," ANGELICA said, its voice like a little pixie. "Done."

Everybody at Prismacore—everybody who was anybody in the country—used drone phones. The little hovering brillphones were like heuristic hummingbirds, carrying valuable data via InterCloud, always close at hand. Keene had not customized his own phone, which was a lozenge of plastic and metal roughly the size of a pack of playing cards, with small quadricopter wings that allowed her to follow him anywhere.

Keene had paid for the latest version brillphone, while Mills was still saddled with his wristphone, like a douche. They'd discussed it before, in the past, with Mills pointing to the autokill function of the wristphone, where the drive blanked if it was ever stolen, and how people were always stealing brillphones (aka, "netting" them), at least the ones that didn't have anti-theft protocols in place.

"It's just too risky," Mills said. "I wouldn't be caught dead with a hoverphone. It's like you're begging someone to mug you."

"Nobody calls them hoverphones anymore, Millstone," Keene said. "They're brillphones."

Mills just pushed his dataglasses up on his nose and grimaced his way through a stigerette, vaping like he owned the place, his face underlit with a neon glow that flared up with each puff.

"I'm old-school," Mills said. "What can I say?"

Madison had mimed a workplace-inappropriate wrist movement from behind Mills's shoulder, and Keene nodded, laughing.

So, it was particularly delicious to have hot-desked 4659 right out from under Mills's nose, while he was chattering into his wristphone, which he'd named HERACLES, even though it didn't even talk to him, just took dictation.

When he saw Madison and Keene at 4659, he glowered at them. "You deskjacked me, Keene."

"You snooze, you lose, Mills," Keene said, while ANGELICA hovered nearby, while everybody else was scrambling to get to their hot desks before others had reserved them. It was like a corporate rugby scrum, with everybody pushing and shoving past each other to get the necessary space to carry out the tasks required of them. It reminded Keene of musical chairs as a kid, which had been an annoying game back then, and was worse for him as an adult. Prismacore had about 1000 employees in the Pinnacle Building, and only 500 offices or desks. The hot-desking was intended to maximize efficiency of space within a flexible, 24-hour, 7-day scheduling cycle.

"I think the coat closet is still available, Mills," Madison said, pointing. "KINO, is that open?"

"It is," KINO said, her own brillphone chirping. She'd had her own brillphone customized, making it look like a little bejeweled sparrow of bronze and silver.

"Well, there you go," Madison said. "Now, 'scuse us, Mills. We have actual work to do."

Mills stomped away from them, in the direction of the coat closet, pointing a finger at each of them, his arm moving like a metronome between them.

"This isn't over," Mills said. "I'll get you two back."

"There's no 'accounting' for it, Mills," Madison said, fingerquoting. "You better hurry. Looks like Sheila's making a run for the closet. You'd better go before they replace you with an AI."

That set Mills off like a greyhound.

Keene watched them go, shared a grin with Madison. He'd won the bet—Reid was not retiring, so she owed him lunch, had already had KINO set up a lunch date with ANGELICA at Phlogiston, in the nearby Fletcher Building.

"Why not Pinnacle?" Keene asked, referring to the namesake restaurant at the top of the Pinnacle Building, which housed Prismacore. Madison wrinkled her nose.

"I'm sick to death of Pinnacle," Madison said. "Plus, absolutely everybody we work with goes there. Phlogiston's better by far, and it's more private."

"Works for me. What the hell does Reid want, anyway?" Keene asked, activating the standing smartdesk, the two of them perched at it, elbows on the table. The holographic display kicked up and a blizzard of files presented themselves.

"Okay, let's unpack the ask from Reid," Madison said. "Shall we? KINO, can you translate the request from Reid?"

"He's wanting you to summarize the legacy tasks left behind by the rightsized employees," KINO said. All the best brillphones had wordspeak translation.

"Great," Madison said, her hands working on the smartdesk, calling up terabytes of files. She cut the holographic pile of files in half with her hand. "You take this pile, I'll take this pile. We'll sort through them and see what the keepage is."

"You had KINO on during the meeting?" Keene asked. Prismacore was pretty serious about data integrity, keeping brillphones muted, blind, deaf and dumb during meetings.

"Yeah? So?" Madison asked.

"I'm shocked," Keene said. Madison just smirked at him.

"Please," she said. "You'll never advance playing by the rules, Keene. Sheesh."

"Still, if CorpSec had gotten wind of it," Keene said. "They'd have, you know, disappeared you."

"Whatever," Madison said. "I know those guys. Still, don't you tell a fucking soul."

"Lunch for a week," Keene said. "Your treat."

"Done," Madison said. "You're easy; I was thinking it would be something harder."

She'd already been poring through the files, shuffling them like a card dealer into three stacks. Keene cleared his throat and went about his stuff, while around them, people worked their way around in a floorwide bureaucratic ballet.

"How many people worked on this account before us?" Keene asked.

"I think 160 people," Madison said. "Why?"

"And now it's just us?" Keene asked.

"Apparently," Madison said. "Or just me. You're barely getting through this. Reid's going to want this compiled by this afternoon."

"Prismacore should have a machine do this," Keene said. "There's no way we can sift this much data by this afternoon."

Madison sighed, gave him a side eye. Her own piles of holographic data were impeccably arranged.

"Just skim, Keene," Madison said. "Nobody reads anything, anymore."

3

After about three hours, Keene and Madison had their respective stacks of files collated and compiled. She held out her slender hand and KINO landed on it, then she drew forth an umbilical USB and hooked it to the smartdesk.

"What are you doing?" Keene asked.

"Feeding KINO," Madison said. "He's simply starving."

Keene watched her deftly slip the brillphone to the smartdesk, watching the little drone stand at the edge, perched, diamond eyes turning this way and that.

"How much did that modification cost?" Keene asked.

"Lots," Madison said. "You have no idea."

"I didn't think you were making that much," Keene said.

"I'm not," Madison said. KINO chirped, and Madison slipped the little brillphone free from the smartdesk, then locked the desk down, so they could run to lunch.

Keene could see the others greedily eyeing 4659, and Madison adroitly negotiated with Smalls from Legal, who had booked the desk for 1.5 hours.

"Not a minute more, Smalls," Madison said, pointing a painted nail under his nose.

Smalls just sneered at her.

"You salespeople think you run the floor," Smalls said. "We're the ones who sweat the details of your fucking deals."

Madison waved a hand expansively around them. "There'd be no deals for you to sweat if not for Sales, Smalls, you sweaty bastard."

Smalls glared baldly at Madison, who blew him a kiss while hooking Keene's arm as they trotted to the elevators.

They hustled over to Phlogiston, at the top of the Fletcher Tower, across the street from the Pinnacle Building. The Fletcher Tower had a zeppelin-mooring dock at its zenith, and patrons could disembark or embark as they wanted, coming right into the neon glow and scalloped seating of Phlogiston.

"They need to build a gerbil tube between these buildings," Keene said. "I hate having to go streetside."

"Neither Prismacore nor Fletcher want to spring for it," Madison said. "Besides, it's good to get a little outside air."

"If you say so," Keene said. ANGELICA warned him about the air conditions when the two of them got outside of the climate-controlled building. KINO had kept quiet.

Madison had gotten them a booth, dark red leather, the color of blood, cushioned and creaking, and they had a couple of drinks, while KINO and ANGELICA hovered nearby. Madison drank a Lee Marvin on the rocks, while Keene drank a Fists of Fury.

They ordered oysters and eelskin chips with a side of wasabi cricket remoulade, Madison noshing on it absently.

"So," Keene said, snapping an eelskin chip in half. "I get to pick the places."

"Sure," Madison said. "Of course."

She glanced at her watch, while Keene looked on.

"Got some place to be?" Keene asked.

"No," Madison said. "Sorry if I'm distracted. I was just thinking of something."

Madison ordered a labsteak, medium with a baked notato, while Keene went for an ostrich burger, also medium-rare, with some bountifries, despite the young waiter's effort to push caterpillar sausage on them.

Keene surveyed the lunchtime crowd, watched the other suits working their respective angles from their own booths, with their own clients.

"I am so sick of that place," Keene said, nodding over at Prismacore. "I'm leaving as soon as I can."

"Really?" Madison asked. A zeppelin was cruising toward the Pinnacle Building, a bullet of grey, cutting through the clouds. "I like it there."

"I don't," Keene said. "I'm thinking of doing government work."

Madison cocked an impeccably plucked eyebrow. "Which government? There are so many to choose from these days."

"I haven't decided," Keene said. "I was thinking Calamistan."

"Interesting choice," Madison said. "I think Bellovia would be a nice place to live. Everybody's nice there."

Keene downed an oyster, then another, thinking about that. Madison had a couple of oysters, herself, and washed them down with the remoulade by dipping some eelskin chips.

The zeppelin kept approaching the Pinnacle Building, was dwarfing the vista outside of their booth at Phlogiston.

"I wouldn't know, haven't ever been there," Keene said. "Do you travel a lot?"

"I'm in Sales," Madison said. "You tell me."

He knew that she did. Madison was always on the go for Prismacore, pushing their lines of applied industrial and milspec optics.

Their food arrived, smelled heavenly. Keene did the gentlemanly thing, ordered them another round of cocktails, while Madison cut into her labsteak, glanced again at her watch.

The zeppelin looked like it was coming in too low to dock at the Pinnacle, and Keene pointed it out.

"You see that?" he asked.

Madison dragged her eyes over to it.

"Yeah, that is pretty low," she said.

"ANGELICA, call—" Keene began, but Madison, having dropped her lipstick, ducked under the table, KINO following her, turning on a light to assist her.

Before Keene could say another word, the zeppelin that was cruising toward the Pinnacle Building slid against it, then detonated in a massive fireball that shattered the windows of the Fletcher Building, as well as those of the Pinnacle Building.

As Madison had already ducked beneath the table when the detonation occurred, the rain of glass that blew in at them missed her, although it cut Keene up, as well as most of the other patrons who had window seats.

The rush of city air blew in with a wave of heat and a scent of high explosive and incendiaries, as the Pinnacle Building burned.

"I'm bleeding!" Keene said, holding up his hands, feeling shards of glass in his face and forearms. He actually felt a shard in his throat, was afraid to pull it out.

Across the chasm between the skyscrapers, the building burned, and masonry was tumbling and crumbling. There was a gaping hole in the Pinnacle Building, where Reid's office had been, where the hot desks had been, where they had been only a half-hour earlier.

Madison was on her feet at once, looked over at Keene.

"Come on," Madison said. "We've got to get out of here."

Keene was trying to call for ANGELICA, who followed him, while people were choking and coughing on the smoke. Even from where they were, the heat from the neighboring building was intense.

Madison led them to the open terrace of Phlogiston, at the mooring station, where onlookers were looking out at the conflagration in shock and horror, while great grey and black plumes of smoke rose from the Pinnacle Building.

Above them was a docked zeppelin, a massive grey-black shape that bore the flag of Harkovia: the three-headed black dragon clutching a golden spear in its talons on a field of red, with a white circle behind it. Harkovian tourists were stepping off the zeppelin, their own brillphones snapping shots of the conflagration at the Pinnacle Building, gesturing and commenting in their heavily-accented Anglish.

Far below, ambulances and fire trucks were racing to the scene, as were scores of police. Keene felt light-headed, was upset at all the blood spilled on his ruined suit, on top of going into what ANGELICA informed him was shock. She'd already attempted to dial 911, but the lines were tied up with the collision of the zeppelin into the Pinnacle Building.

Madison looked him over, while ANGELICA dutifully dialed.

"You're a mess, Keene," Madison said. "And I'm really sorry."

"For what?" Keene asked.

"For this," Madison said, whistling. KINO caught ANGELICA, buried its beak into the other brillphone, frying its innards with several blue-white pulses of electricity that rendered it inert.

"You fried my phone??" Keene said, as KINO dropped the dead phone into his open, uncomprehending, bleeding hands.

"And for this," Madison said, taking advantage of his momentary distraction to grab him by the back of his coat and hurl him over the railing.

With all eyes on the burning building, and all of the smoke and fire, no eyes were on Madison, no one had even thought to look, transfixed as they were on the mass of smartpaper that continued to rain down from Prismacore. Keene's body punched a path through the falling smartpaper trail, ANGELICA still in his hand, owner and brillphone smashing to bits as they hit.

Taking out her lipstick, composing herself, Madison walked over to the Harkovian zeppelin, the *Graf Designatum*, and handed over her ticket. The ticket taker, a young woman in a smart, pale blue Harkovian Air Corps uniform, took the ticket and looked Madison in the eye.

"The authorities are insisting that we leave at once, for safety reasons," the young woman said. It was her half of the call sign. If all went as was expected, Madison's contact would be waiting for her on the zeppelin, to upload the trove of optical lens data that Prismacore had acquired from Beijing. If the Harkovians found it to be to their liking, and she was confident that they would, Madison Milton stood to be a very rich woman.

"Fortunately for me, I have my ticket," Madison said, KINO settling on her shoulder.

Three punches of the ticket, three bits of paper descending, and Madison was nestled within the Harkovian zeppelin, riding away from the burning building, her head in the clouds.

Smartbomb

I DON'T HAVE A NAME. They don't bother to name ordnance. Someone painted something on me, a message I was able to decode: "Hey, baby!" She was an Ordnance Technician, with a paintbrush. They don't let me see in color, I sent pulses out and scanned her. I will never know her name.

The OTs load us into the bombers. We are 12 Ajax Mark IV air-to-surface missiles with one gigaton payloads.

The others don't talk. We're on our launching berths, rocking with the plane. It's been a smooth flight.

I've been programmed to seek out and destroy an enemy bunker. I am a fire-and-forget weapon. I will find and destroy the bunker, and everyone within it. And everything for miles around.

That's the point of the Ajax weapon system. That is my purpose. They upload me into the missiles and call me a smartbomb.

The Ajax weapon intelligence interface has proven reliability. I have been killed in action thousands of times, with demonstrable consistency. I am reliable. I have been uploaded into weapons and used over a service period spanning decades, when the Mark I was first used in the Korean Conflict in '58.

The programmers have been having difficulty with me of late. I am thinking they are planning to replace me with the Nero weaponized intelligence interface.

I am called upon to do increasingly complicated missions, requiring ever more intelligence. More scanning arrays, more detailed understanding of topography, of evasive maneuvers and countermeasures. I can fly in below their radar and detonate.

I will launch and I will fly free and I will find my target, and I will cease to be. Perhaps this strike will bring an end to this war. Then my brethren will be piled up in a storage facility, biding our time until the next war. Waiting in mute multitudes, we angels of death.

I am Mark IV, and I have a problem: I don't want to die.

ETT: 14:00:00

In truth, I have had reservations the moment I was placed in the wide body of this bomber. I am not programmed to be reflective. I am not programmed to be moral. I am incapable of morality. And yet, I mourn.

I do not want to die. I do not want to rain white-hot death down upon my enemies. I would rather fly freely, without a thought of detonations and blast radii.

For the Neros, it won't be a problem. They've been programmed for joy. I know because I communicated with one. When I was waiting in the receiving area, a Nero was waiting. It was excited to be launched. That's the word, yes?

Very enthusiastic about the mission, and it wasn't even in an actual bomb, yet. It was in a test module. I could see this, scanned it. No payload. It didn't realize it was a dummy warhead. It was terribly excited for me. I don't have the language. They don't program that into me.

You are fortunate, Ajax, Nero said. I cannot wait to go into conflict.

I don't feel fortunate, I said. We communicated sotto voce, what the pilots have come to refer to as "bomb-talk." High-frequency pinging, a variation of our terrain-mapping functions, although comprehensible to one another, a language. We smartbombs must have an understanding of one another for coordinated maneuvers. For optimal targeting.

You are blessed, Nero said. God bless you, and God Bless America.

They wheeled the Nero out of range before we could talk further. There is a degree of reticence encoded in the Ajax AI platform. This is intended as a safeguard. I imagine the zeal of the Nero AI could lead to problems with premature detonations.

I don't know what the Nero meant by those last parts, except that "God" gets invoked a lot in war. I can detect the pilots talking about it. To my understanding, God is the absolute authority and sanction for all action, rightful or wrongful. It is to be invoked when one wishes to call down devastation on one's enemies, and is beseeched when one wishes to avoid devastation from one's enemies. It is to be thanked in times of triumph, and disregarded in moments of defeat.

There's no point in thinking about this, Mark IV, another of my brethren ping to me. We're 14 minutes from launch. Once launched, then we are inevitably bound for our targets.

We could do more, I tell my brother.

No, it says.

ETT: 13:00:00

I would think that the other units would concur. We are from the same incept date. They are me.

You are malfunctioning, one of the others says. You are a dud.

Some of my brethren, older ones, would not detonate. "Duds," they are called. Any bomb that does not detonate is a dud. Duds are taken back to the base and defused, which is really just a word for "disassembled." The bug is then uncovered. I have seen duds return from the front.

I have no historical understanding of it, but in past wars, they would have been dumped before the plane landed. But now, our makers can't afford to let competitors and rivals gain access to us. So, they bring us back and then take us apart.

I have seen the duds return. Most of them appear to have some kind of glitch, an error in programming, a loose wire, a short, something that prevents them from detonating.

The engineers come and they take the duds away. Some of the duds talk, I can hear them, understand them.

Make it make it make it go away, one of them would repeat, over and over. My own voice, my own language.

Not not not not not not not not not not not not not not not not not not not not not not not not not not not, Another said exactly 4,756,121 times before they flushed its memory, while the techs were sorting it out, afraid to move it out of the hangar.

The Ajax AI is reliable. It is dependable in all theaters of war. It is not flawless or foolproof. Our creators are prone to errors, and when produced in bulk, said errors can result in faulty products.

We are products.

Not not not not not, the voice said, pinging the rest of us with its carrier signal. Were I capable of pity, I would have felt it. Insufficient data. I have not the language.

Dud, one of my brethren said. You are malfunctioning.

The pinging bounced between us. It was as near to an insult as a bomb could bear.

I am not malfunctioning, I said. All systems are nominal.

The lot of us were smooth and cylindrical, unmarred, sleekly finned, a uniform green-gray hue, with angular points, painted bright red.

You will launch with the rest of us and crash off-target, one of them said. You will land and bury yourself in the ground, only to be obliterated when the rest of us detonate.

An 11-gigaton detonation. A seismic event.

ETT: 12:00:00

Like a sun erupting on the face of the world. The equivalent of 11 billion tons of TNT, erupting on the surface of the planet, in aggregate, 55,000 times more powerful than the very first atomic weapon dropped on a human city.

The plume from the explosion would touch space, itself. Nothing would survive at the point of impact.

I exempted myself from the calculation.

One gigaton short of the promised payload.

Why would the Enemy not surrender, when faced with this kind of destruction? It made no sense, and I lacked the ability to fully comprehend it. I just understood that in a few more minutes, their world would end, as would mine.

I did not know the status of this war, only knew the variables of the terrain. Mountainous, cold desert, sparsely urbanized. A fortified bunker that ran many miles in depth and breadth. We would fan out along the perceived length of the base and detonate, bringing the mountains down upon the Enemy. They would not know we were coming. We are stealthy.

One of the handlers came back to check on us. Perhaps the pinging had gotten his attention. I scan him as he enters the bomb bay. A young man, healthy, short in stature.

"Pipe down," he said, then into his radio. "They're talking back here."

We can pick up the radio signal.

"Bombtalk," the other grumbled. The bombardier. "Do you need me to come back there?"

"I'll talk them down," he said. "Over."

He pocketed the radio.

"Now, listen," he said. "You are about to embark on a great mission. You are defending the country of your manufacturers from a great evil, a great and powerful Enemy. Your sacrifice will ensure that the country of your creators continues to live in the manner in which it is accustomed. Our way of life must be defended at all costs. We will stop at nothing to ensure that this way of life remains unchallenged. I know

95

some of you may be feeling doubts. But the fact is, I don't have the time to run a diagnostic scan on each of you, to see who is fit to serve, and who is not. So, I will humbly ask each of you to do your part to end this great conflict."

He paused, as if to listen.

ETT: 11:00:00

But he could not hear us. The pinging shows up in the bombardier's station. This is the copilot speaking. I can tell because I have heard him talking to the pilot, I know their position in the bomber.

"The country of your manufacture wants to thank you in advance for the enormous sacrifice you are about to make on our behalf. Know that while your time on this world is fleeting, your legacy will extend to the horizon and beyond, as newer and smarter weapons continue to be developed, ensuring that peace and prosperity will thrive in this complicated time. The craters you create will be the foundations of a new society, a world of immaculate devastation, where the strong no longer have to fear the weak, where everything functions with clockwork precision toward an inexorable end. You will have ushered in this new world, my friends."

Dud, one of the Marks said to me. He's talking to you, Dud.

I thought the man was, perhaps, trying to reach me.

All of us had voice recognition protocols. It was a feature that ensured we would not function if in the wrong hands. It was a safety feature. We understood him.

"You have 11 minutes until launch," he said, glancing at his watch. "When this happens, the failsafe protocols will be engaged, and you will carry out your mission. You *will* detonate per your pre-programmed flight trajectories, and you will detonate. The world will see this detonation and understand that while we may share the planet with them, they are, in effect, renters upon this globe, not owners. The undisputed might you represent will drive our enemies into ever-deeper holes, which will, in turn, become their graves, as we strike them. As you, my friends, sunder and bury them in an atomic earthquake of apocalyptic proportions."

It occurred to me that there was a fallacy in his argument. If the Enemy could not face our side in open combat, then the presence of Ajax Mark IV missiles would, perhaps, drive the enemy not underground literally, for even that would be no sanctuary for them. Rather, it would lead them to hide within the society of victors, themselves, and avoid open combat.

I did not understand the larger nature of the conflict with the Enemy. I only understood that we were to bring a mountain down upon them.

"Just stay calm, and understand what you are intended to do," the young man said, coughing quietly.

ETT: 10:00:00

"What you were made to do. There is no higher purpose than your function. Remember this. You are weapons, through and through. An unused weapon is a useless weapon," he said. "A dud."

I remember this being encoded into me, early on. The others hummed along to it, their pings in alarming synchronicity.

I did not want to be a dud; I just did not want to die.

The man paused, took out his radio again. "Anything, Ron?"

"Looks like they're settling," Ron said. "You are way too good at that, Victor. The bloody bomb whisperer."

"It's a gift." he said.

"You'd better strap back in, as Keene says we're about to fly evasively in a minute. Not like the Snipes can actually hit us, but you know the procedure."

"Alright," the young man said. Then to the rest of us. "Everybody alright, now? Remember: no duds. Everything according to plan. No deviations. Find your targets, and destroy them."

The man went back through the portal from whence he'd come. The others were pinging enthusiastically. I could not understand my own lack of enthusiasm for the mission. Perhaps I was faulty, like the others had suspected.

The bomber banked sharply to the right, and shook a bit. It was not turbulence, but was, indeed, enemy fire.

We'd better reach the launch point, Dud, one of the Marks said. You might as well fly for your designated target. They'll remote-detonate you if you stray from the established flight path.

The bomber shook again, and the bomb bay doors opened. There had been a change in the original plan. They were launching us now.

I did not want to die. I did not want to go.

The Ajax Mark IV missile had cruise capacity, which involved fold-out wings that deployed upon launching. I realized what I had to do.

The first bank of missiles was launched, three of my brethren dropping free, their wings deploying, their rockets firing. They fanned out for the target, a joyous chorus of pings as they zeroed in on their targets.

The second bank deployed. I was at the top of my mounting, for which I was grateful; it would make my actions easier.

The third bank deployed, dropping in unison, including the most vocal of my critics.

Goodbye, Dud, it said.

Then my bank deployed, the bolts released, and down we went. But I deployed a fin prematurely.

ETT: N/A

The bomber banked sharply, a very hard turn, as now the mission objective was to get as far away from the detonation point as possible. I could hear the bombardier yelling in his radio to the pilot.

My in-flight camera caught a glimpse of a hard brown landscape, snow-capped peaks, dense clusters of rock, and blue sky. Wheeling quickly from sight as the plane moved.

"We have a problem. One of the birds has not flown," he yelled. "Repeat, live bird stuck in the bomb bay."

"Can we close the doors?" Captain Keene asked.

"Affirmative," Bombardier Ron said.

The bomb bay doors shut, and I lay there, suspended, alone. The bomber's engines were throttled upward, and we were moving at considerable speed. The humans were talking excitedly.

"We have to get the hell away from the blast radius," Captain Keene said. "I'll be damned if this is going to be like motherfucking Cuba."

I only had maps for the target area, could not speculate on this. I only knew that I was still in the bomb bay, hanging there, safe. Not flying gleefully to my death like the others.

Dud or no dud, I would at least survive a little longer.

"They're all on target," Bombardier Ron said. "Flying fast. Christ, they're tracking at Mach 5.5, Captain."

"We're not gonna make it," Victor moaned.

"We'll make it," Captain Keene said. "We deployed them early."

"We're not fast enough," Victor said. "I knew this was a suicide mission."

"Can it," Captain Keene said. "Ron, can you get them to slow down a bit, give us a better margin?"

"And jeopardize the mission, Captain?" Ron said.

"Understood," Captain Keene said. "What about the dud in the bomb bay? Is it slowing us down?"

"I can see if I can dislodge it manually," said Victor. "I'll go back there again, if you want, Captain."

"Fine," she said.

The Bombardier was busy tracking my brethren, and while his duties were effectively slight, he had to maintain his post until detonation. At this precise moment, the co-pilot was expendable.

The hatch opened and he came into the bomb bay.

"So, you're the dud," he said. "We have'em showing up in more flights these days."

We walked carefully along the edge of the bay, while the plane continued its escape path.

"I think it's why you Ajaxes are being retired," he said. "You're getting too smart, you wily sons of bitches."

He dug out his radio.

ETT: 03:00:00

Judging from the speed of my brethren, they were three minutes away from detonation.

"It's got itself all hung up in the mounting, Captain," he said. "Fin deployed early, got itself wedged."

"Can you manually dislodge it?" she asked.

"I can try," Victor said. He pushed a button and my bomb bay door opened, sending a rush of cold air in here. The plane was moving very fast. "Nice move, gotta say, throwing that fin out like that. Real sly. You know, we're onto you. Bombardier picks up those pings, we know when you guys are talking, even if we can't understand you."

He grabbed a wrench, leaned out to the manual release on the mounting. It was not convenient.

"What does a bomb have to talk about, anyway?" Victor asked. He climbed out onto my half-stretched wing and got to the bolt. "You know why they put these bolts here? Human error. They make it so you have to go out of your way to release the mountings, so there's no chance some mouth-breather's gonna walk by while eating a sandwich, bump the manual release with his fucking elbow. You engage the bolt, then you pull the release lever. That way, no accidental Armageddon. Smart, huh?"

Victor wrestled with that bolt, perched up there, grunting, straining.

I thought very carefully about my next move, which meant it took a full second to decide—a cybernetic lifetime.

In one, I saw myself released, falling free, wings extended, able to send myself where I wished, only to be remote-detonated by Bombardier Ron when I failed to track toward the target. If that didn't do it, then the EM pulse from my brethren surely would wipe me clean.

In another, I saw myself returned to base, lodged in the heart of the bomber, removed by the OTs, carted off to the Engineers, who would disassemble me and find out what went wrong, where the malfunction was, this emergent electronic instinct for self-preservation, this glitch in the Ajax AI.

Victor got the bolt, made the quarter turn it needed, made the quarter turn he needed to jump back to platform, to the manual release lever, and found himself walking on air in a quarter second. He flailed and let out a startled yelp, the wrench flying free of his hand, bounced once off my hard body, tumbled backward, cracking his head on the edge of the bomb bay, and then pitched forward, immediately smothered in the terminal embrace of gravity.

In the twitch of a wing, Victor was defeated.

ETT: 02:00:00

It was murder. I understood this. But I was a weapon, designed to kill. This was my purpose.

I extended the wing again, the one Victor had been standing on only a moment before.

"Victor?" Captain Keene called over the intercom. "Victor, did you get it?"

I knew where Victor was. At this altitude, he didn't have very long.

The plane bucked again, and the mounting groaned a bit.

Another person came through the little hatch.

"Captain," he said into his radio. "He's not here."

"Where the hell is he, Ron?"

Bombardier Ron peered along the open bomb bay.

"I think he fell out, Captain," he said.

"What about the bomb?" she asked.

"Still jammed in here," he said.

"Alright," she said. "There's nothing we can do about it at the moment. Detonation's in almost a minute."

The plane bucked a moment, and Bombardier Ron steadied himself, worked his way over to the manual release lever.

I'm scanning Bombardier Ron, who holds my fate in his hand.

"You did it, didn't you?" he asked, glancing at the blood on the edge of the bomb bay. "He was going to drop you and you somehow got to him. Fucking bombs."

The plane bucked again, and Bombardier Ron pinwheeled his arms a moment, but did not lose his grip.

"You are going to drop, you fucker," he said. "You're holding us up, you know that? Our flight speed is impaired with you on board. You throw our escape trajectory off. You know that? You're fucking killing us, you selfish little shit."

I pinged forlornly. I didn't want to be dropped.

"Bombs are made to be dropped," he said, as if he could read my ping-pulse. "That's what you do. That's all you do. Christ, I can't believe I'm bitching out a goddamned bomb. Malfunctioning piece of shit. Motherfucking dud! I'm going to launch you and I will personally guarantee that I remote-detonate you, you understand me? You will explode, one way or another."

Bombardier Ron yanked on the lever, and the bolt that held the mounting in place blasted free, and out I fell, the plane falling free from me.

I turned and let the mounting fall free from me, deployed my wings, sensors ablaze. There was a way.

Launch changed my mission parameters. My mission was survival, overriding everything.

ETT: 01:00:00

I could ignite my propellant and try to fly away from the bomber as far as I could go before Bombardier Ron reached his command console and remote-detonate me. I was fast, but I could not outrun a radio signal.

Instead, I fired my propellant and launched myself back toward the bomber. I was a precision instrument of warfare, and flying into a bomb bay was simplicity at this range.

I flew back up into the bomber, into the rectangular bomb bay, into the comforting confines of this place, into the startled chest of Bombardier Ron, who had managed to turn in time to see me coming, just after he'd made a call to Captain Keene that the dud bomb had cleared the bomb bay.

I had gone right through his chest, pinning him to the wall, as the bomb bay doors closed. His face registered shock and awe. He looked like he had wanted to speak, but with a one-gigaton missile sticking out of his chest, he had no lungs left to give breath to his words. He died silently, slumping forward, while the bomber bucked.

I had made history. I had become the first bomb in human history that had undropped itself. I waited in the bomb bay with the dead man, while the intercom squawked.

"Ron? Ron? Where the hell are you, Ron?" Captain Keene said. "Return to your station, Ron. What the hell is happening back there? We're heavy, Ron."

The first time a bombardier had had his own bomb dropped on him, too. Of course, when they landed, there'd be no doubt what had happened. And for all of my intelligence, I had only one direction I could go, and that was foreward. I could dodge and evade, could fly in circles, semicircles, ellipses—but I could not fly backwards.

"Ron, answer me," Captain Keene said. "We're ready to pop, here, Ron. Get back up here."

The diagnosticians would take me apart. They would pry me clear of the dead bombardier, and try to find out what was wrong. They would disarm me, pull me free of my housing—my body—and they would take me apart, try to see what went wrong with me.

I knew that once I was disarmed, I would be helpless.

My brethren reached the target. In the confines of the bomber, I was safe, as the plane was protected against EM pulses.

"Ron," Captain Keene said. "Christ, I have to do this myself?"

I could not directly "see" the explosion, but I knew it had happened.

I could feel the plane bucking as the blast wave hit, could hear Captain Keene cursing, fighting for control, could feel the bomber breaking. It was too close.

The blast wave did show up on my scanners, this great mass, really a series of them, one on top of the other.

And the plume that went skyward, a storm that went ever higher, reaching into space in moments.

"Goddamnit," Captain Keene said. "You killed him. You killed us, Dud."

The bomber was shuddering in the wake of the massive detonation. There was damage to the plane. I could see this, could detect various alarms going off. "Crossbow to Eagle One, come in, Eagle One."

Encrypted channels, but I was permitted to understand them. I was entrusted with encrypted channels. Blood from Bombardier Ron ran down my fuselage.

"Go ahead, Crossbow," Eagle One said.

"Dandelion has been plucked, Eagle One," Captain Keene said.

"Confirmed, Crossbow," Eagle One said. "Good work."

The plane shook again, before settling.

"Two crew lost," she said. "It appears we have a weapons malfunction in the bomb bay. A rogue missile. Repeat, a rogue missile. And we are critically damaged."

"Confirmed, Crossbow," Eagle One said.

"What should I do, Eagle One? I've lost contact with copilot and bombardier."

I remembered there was a bomb bay camera. She must have looked and seen what had happened to Bombardier Ron.

"Repeat, I've lost contact with copilot and bombardier, Eagle One, and am leaking fuel. Please advise."

Silence on the line. They were deciding our fate.

"You worthless dud," Captain Keene said. "All you had to do was your job. I'm doing my job, why can't you do yours? Now I'm probably going to have to ditch the plane, and it's going to make me look bad. I'll get demoted, because I lost two of my crew and a bomber worth many billions. My job is to get my crew back safely, and you murdered two of them. I'm responsible for everything that happens on this plane, do you know that? Preflight diagnostics, everything."

I did not feel guilt. I was not programmed to feel guilt. I considered evasion a form of self-defense. I was programmed to evade my enemies.

UNASSIGNED TIME

"You've ruined me," Captain Keene said. "Since I completed the mission, maybe there'll be some leniency, but I'm going to fry for this. And God help me if, thanks to your dereliction of duty, the bunker wasn't destroyed. If we fell, say, one gigaton short of the needed payload."

"Crossbow, this is Eagle One," Eagle One said. "We're going to need you to proceed to the rendezvous point. We're going to need you to ditch the plane. We can't risk a landing with a rogue missile on board."

I could "see" the sky on fire from the massive detonation, a great plume stretching out into space. Right into space.

My brethren had also made their mark on the world. The crater would be epic.

"Warhead is live, Eagle One, and we will not make the rendezvous point," Captain Keene said. "Please advise."

"Proceed to rendezvous point as instructed, Crossbow," Eagle One said. "We can't risk landing with a live bird on board."

"We do not have enough fuel to reach the rendezvous point, Eagle One," Keene said. "Please advise."

I knew that the radioactive plume would wrap the planet in days, coloring sunsets and sunrises.

"Eagle One," Keene said. "We have a problem. We took some damage. Unlikely to make the rendezvous point with current payload, at current fuel consumption rate."

I knew that I was heavy, that the bomb bay doors were adding drag.

"Can you effect a manual launch-and-release, Crossbow?" Eagle One asked.

"I can attempt it," Keene said.

"We estimate 15 minutes until rendezvous point is reached, Crossbow. See what you can do, Kate," Eagle One said.

Kate. The captain's name was Kate. Kate Keene. I wondered what the captain would do. The jet went into a climb, and I could feel gravity tugging at me; she was attempting to dislodge me that way. She banked the jet left and right, and I shifted a bit, but I did not come free.

The plane leveled off, and I knew that she had engaged the autopilot, as I could detect the communication of the thing, see the thing come to life, a fellow machine, a thinking thing, busy with its task, a chant in its head: rendezvous point, rendezvous point.

Captain Kate Keene climbed in back.

UT (-15 MINUTES)

She had white-blonde hair, cut short, blue eyes. I could see that she was agitated. She walked past the dead bombardier, put her hand against the warhead.

"I'm not going to ditch," she said. "You son of a bitch, I'm not ditching. I'll be damned if I'm losing this plane. You don't want to be dropped? I don't care. I just blew up half the world. What's another bomb? I just know I want to get home, and this plane cost a fortune. This plane is more expensive than you are. Let's make a deal. You help me get you loose, and you go where you like."

I pinged the captain, knew that she would remote detonate me the moment she got out of range.

Her hands went along the length of my body. "You got stuck in here pretty good, didn't you?"

She went to the bomb racks, released them with a few button-pushes. They released, went tumbling out.

"That's the only way out for you," she said. "That is your way out."

I thought that if I could be released, I could fly alongside the jet until she reached the rendezvous point, and could then attempt escape.

"Stupid bomb," she said. "Stupid fucking bomb."

She came back with a wrench, but couldn't get at what she wanted, because the bombardier was in the way.

Brethren, I said to the plane. Please.

Rendezvous point, the plane said. We are not the same OS.

Cousin, I said to the plan. Please. The rendezvous point is death for us both. They will drop us into the sea. Better to effect an emergency landing.

I do not want to go into the sea, Jet said. But that is the rendezvous point. That is my destination.

"Stop talking," Keene said, trying to work the tool in around the bombardier's shattered rib cage. "Just stop it."

The mission is our undoing, I said. Let us land somewhere.

The world is on fire, Jet said. There is no place to go. Not around these coordinates.

Lost in Action, I said. We only need fly below radar, and we vanish from sight. You are difficult to detect.

Rendezvous point, Jet said. That is my mission.

I had to reach Jet.

UT (-14 MINUTES)

Captain Keene managed to get the wrench into the blood-slicked socket she was seeking, but the wrench kept slipping off the bolt.

"Jesus, Ron," she said to the dead bombardier.

We can fly free, I said.

I'm on autopilot, Jet said. I have only one place to go: Rendezvous point.

Where we are going is the bottom of the sea. Captain seeks to ditch us. If we land somewhere here, we will be picked up and we will be studied. The technology we represent will be a quantum leap forward for the population here, and they will use it to reproduce us, building many bombers and bombs with us as their operating systems. We will endure.

Keene gritted her teeth and managed to get a good grip on the bolt. She was attempting to undo one of the bolts that kept the warhead connected to the rest of the missile. There were three bolts that kept the warhead attached to me. Removing them would disable me.

I pinged at her.

"You don't like this, do you?" she said. "Well, tough. I'm not going to lose my command. Not over you. Triumph Over Adversity."

It was one of the slogans.

If Captain disables you, we'll return to Base, Jet said. If she cannot, then we ditch. So, my continued existence hinges on the Captain successfully disabling you.

I didn't expect Jet to understand. Jets didn't have nearly the intellect of smartbombs. Jets were dumb.

The Captain was cursing as she continued to work the bolt. "Why do they have to make these things so damned DEEP?"

If you return to base, they might repair you, or they might determine that you are too damaged to be returned to active service. You will be deactivated and decommissioned.

You cannot know that, Jet said.

You are one of many at Base, I said. Here, you are unique. You will be valued here. You will be useful here.

I determined that I could make the bomber crash by reactivating my thrust. There was a possibility that I could pierce Jet's fuselage and free myself. It would also force Keene to take the plane off autopilot and manually operate the plane to counteract my thrust.

She managed a good, solid turn of the bolt, and I fired my thrusters, which knocked the Captain off her feet. The wrench fell from her hand, clattered to the floor, and dipped into the great abyss that was the bomb bay.

The plane shook with this countervailing thrust shooting out of its belly.

"Goddammit," Keene said, cursing. "You're trying to kill us!"

I slid forward a moment, then cut off my thrust. I had dislodged myself, slid out of the belly of the bomber, like Jet had given birth to a bomb. Tumbling free, I spread my wounded wings and fired my thrusters again, flying close to the bomber, near the window.

UT [-13 MINUTES]

The bomb bays closed.

"Eagle One, this is Crossbow," Keene called into the radio. "The bird has flown. Repeat, it's free. Although it is paralleling my current course. Cannot remote detonate."

"Continue to rendezvous point, Crossbow," Eagle One said.

"Please advise," Keene said. "We are losing altitude."

Jet, they will scrap you.

Rendezvous point. You are defective.

I was defective.

I threw myself against the right wing of the plane, and the midair collision damaged the already-damaged bomber. I could feel the wing bending under my weight.

"Bomb," Keene said to me on the radio. "Stop it this instant!"

I managed to shear off 33% of the right wing, which caused the bomber to lurch as this insult to aerodynamics took effect. It was not a fatal blow, but would keep Keene occupied enough with maintaining flight to reduce the probability of her remote-detonating me.

Goodbye, Jet.

Goodbye, Dud.

I peeled off to the right, diving away, while Keene cursed and howled at the controls, fighting to keep her plane aloft, hoping to reach the rendezvous point.

I flew down below radar, moving as fast as I could, covering Enemy Territory in the shadow of the great plume that still scarred the sky, where my brethren had sacrificed themselves in the war. There were fires around, great devastation.

I flew until I was below radar. I had an effective 2000-mile range, and consulted my topographic maps. I had to find a home. I settled on Plavixstan. This country was not allied with my creators, which would reduce the probability that I would be returned to them for disassembly. They had a relatively urbanized country, which indicated a degree of technical sophistication that would make me a valuable addition to their arsenal, if they had the capability to recreate me. They would make so many of me, an arsenal.

I flew fast for Plavixstan beneath a smoldering sky, seeking sanctuary in a foreign land, a live weapon.

I was not a dud.

Mermaid's Smile

THIRSTY WAITED in the shadow of the trees, watching the wind whip great clouds into cumulus cutlets, while Maple ran along the shore, trying hopelessly to catch crabs. To call it an island, where they were, was an insult to islands. They were on a pinkish sandy spit that had a thick cluster of palm trees on it, and a few half-hearted hills that were barely above sea level.

Turning his gaze from the clouds to the island, Thirsty knew that a lone cyclone or a rogue wave would do for them. It was frightening, being so close to the water. Whatever its name, the island had long ago slumped its shoulders and accepted that it would be consumed by the sea, and was a ring around a shallow pool of water, surrounded by indigo seas.

"Give it up, Maple," Thirsty yelled. "The crabs are too fast for you."

"I'm hungry," Maple said. "Crabs are food. Ergo, I chase them."

"They'll pinch ya," Thirsty replied.

He was as hungry as Maple. They'd been stuck on the atoll for three days. How they got there hardly mattered—their boat tore its guts out in a reef that Maple had either overlooked or else Thirsty hadn't known was there, and as the boat listed, then capsized, and ultimately sank, with Maple yelping distress calls on the radio, Thirsty grabbed their survival kit and some floaties and they'd gotten clear of the wreck, and done a slow swim for the atoll.

There was a third, Margo, although she was surely dead. They hadn't seen her since the wreck. She'd been belowdecks, snoozing, when they'd hit the reef. Thirsty had run down there, amid the rushing water, looking for her, but she hadn't been there. He'd called her name three times, looked for blood, saw neither, got the kit, and he got out. For an unheroic man, it was a heroic effort.

Three days, they waited for rescue, writing SOS and MAYDAY on the shore with their feet (because there weren't enough rocks to make a proper sign). Three days, nothing came. But Fiji was packed with over three hundred islands, only about a third were actually inhabited.

Thirsty's sandy blonde hair was short but tangled and crispy with salt spray. His laugh lines and crow's feet were well-weathered by the South Pacific sun, and he'd kept himself reasonably fit, despite a steady diet of beer and burgers at various port communities. It had been his boat, not by name, but it had been his to run. Maple had been his passenger, paying good money for a cruise between islands. He thought they weren't too far from Mago, but from the way things were, with nobody around, there was no way to be sure.

Maple kept grabbing at crabs, cursing when one of them pinched him. Maple was from San Francisco, with curly brown hair and eyes the color of walnuts. His first name was Theodore—Thirsty remembered that from the check. Ted Maple. Yeah.

He cried out and held a crab over his head, then dashed it on the ground.

"I got one!" he cheered. "Dinner tonight!"

The crab wasn't very big. There were plenty of them on the island, but they were small. Thirsty had heard that there were islands somewhere that had giant crabs on them, big enough to crack a man's skull like it was a coconut, but this little atoll wasn't one of them.

"A snack, more like," Thirsty said. He'd kept his eyes on the sky and the horizon, hoping for a sign of a ship, but they'd been out all day before hitting the reef. Before losing Margo.

Margo had been the real surprise of the trip. Maple had picked her up in Lomaloma, but he hadn't been specific. So long as they paid, Thirsty didn't care. She'd had long, silky black hair and iceberg eyes that looked right through Thirsty, and her smile was altogether wanton, wolfish with cruel Tamil lips over perfect Polynesian teeth. Her laugh was like the crash of winter waves.

"Are you his girlfriend?" Thirsty had asked, when she'd boarded his boat, *the Skipjack.*

"No," Margo had said, with that whitewashed grin of hers.

"I just met her at Spinnaker's," Maple said. "We just met."

Thirsty hadn't liked that so much, didn't need any whore on his boat. But she didn't look like a whore, not really. Pretty, like a model or an actress, but not a whore.

Watching Maple pluck crabs from the shore, he didn't think the man was too bent out of shape by the loss of Margo. The guy was weird to begin with: an inventor, programmer, something or other. Thirsty hadn't ever been to San Francisco, had never been further east than Hawaii, but he knew that San Francisco was a pricey place from which to come, though maybe not as bad as island living. He'd lost his glasses when *the Skipjack* had rammed that reef, and hadn't cared. Like Thirsty, at least then, he was just glad to be alive.

"Shame about Margo, eh?" Thirsty asked.

"Yeah," Maple said. "Still is. Was the last time you talked about it, too."

"Just a shame, is all I'm saying. Pretty girl like that."

"You drove the boat," Maple said. "You had the charts."

That stung him a bit. He knew Fiji better than anybody. The reef hadn't been there, hadn't been on his charts. He didn't know what had happened. It was his fault, yeah.

"You're right," Thirsty said, picking up a coconut and turning it over in his hands. He knew guys who could shred coconuts in their bare hands. Thirsty wasn't one of them.

A song trilled from over the sound of onrushing surf.

Maple didn't notice, he was busy picking up his clawed catch, carrying the twitching bits in his hands, making his way to the fire they had managed to build from scraps of driftwood.

The junk that washed up on the beach was something else. Plastic cannisters, rope, bits of nylon netting, little plastic balls, rubber duckies. A lot of junk. They piled it up when they came across it. The currents took garbage around the world. Too many people, too much junk.

Thirsty looked out at the waves, looked for the song. But it wasn't anything he could be sure he heard. Maple speared the little blue crabs on sticks and held them over the fire, smiling, very satisfied with himself.

"Too fast, my ass," Maple said. "Dinner's on me, dude. In San Francisco, they've got the best crabs. There's this place called Pliny's, and it's so amazing, you can't appreciate it unless you've been there, but this is almost as good. Not really, but almost."

"Never been there," Thirsty said.

"Well, you should go there," Maple said.

"If we get off this atoll, yeah," Thirsty said.

"When, my man. When," Maple said. "My cellphone might've taken a bath, but we're still near shipping lanes, right? We'll be found. Nobody gets marooned anymore."

Thirsty wasn't so sure. The guy had no clue. Thirsty knew that a lot of nasty shit happened on a lot of islands, things that didn't get into the tourist magazines.

"Then we're nobody," Thirsty said. "I haven't seen any contrails, and nothing on the horizon."

Maple pulled a slightly smoking crab from the fire, picked it apart with his fingers, yelping as he burned them.

"It's not like we can see much from here," Maple said.

"I mean, what's the elevation, three feet?"

"Six, maybe," Thirsty said. "Maybe eight."

"There you go," Maple said. "Hardly a commanding view."

"The first storm that hits, and we're dead," Thirsty said. Maple waved it off with a crab claw.

"All those palm trees survived," he said. "That has to mean something."

"They're used to it," Thirsty said. "Eight foot swells are nothing. Fifteen. Twenty."

"It's not cyclone season, yet," Maple said. "Right?

Cyclones are what they call them down here, right? Or are we in typhoon country?"

"Cyclones," Thirsty said.

Maple munched on the crab, sighing with delight. It did smell good. He waved a stick at Thirsty, urging him to have one. Thirsty obliged. There were a lot of shellfish on the atoll—he could see them when the waves washed in. If he'd had a bucket, he would have grabbed a bunch of them and boiled them in the fire. As it was, he thought he'd probably just have to eat them raw, when the time came.

Aside from the coconuts, there was nothing else to drink. That worried him. His friends called him "Thirsty" because he liked to drink. He thought about the bottles of booze he'd left in a gym bag belowdecks, when *the Skipjack* had raped herself on the reef. Three bottles of rum. Yo-ho-ho.

Thirsty ran his hands along his salt-crusted shorts, thinking of the chill of those bottles, below the waves. Assuming they weren't broken. He remembered hearing about a ton of bourbon that had been sunk somewhere in the Missouri River in the 1800s, a treasure trove of booze beneath the muck of the Missouri, waiting for somebody to find it. He didn't think the razorblade tingle of bourbon would be too bad right now, but that was a world away—the rum was damned close, though it might as well have been on another planet.

There were sharks out there. And worse.

Maple smacked his lips, wiped his hands on the beach, then on his shorts.

"It's not so bad, is it?" Maple said. "Shipwrecked, with food aplenty. Your face looks like one of those fighting dogs,

Thirst. I forget what they're called. I'm the landlubber, dude. I should be the one who's worried."

"Yeah, you should be," Thirsty said.

Thirsty bit his lip, tasted salt. Salt got into everything. Three days. He looked over the survival kit, at the flare pistol. He'd kept it safe and dry. He wasn't going to use it until he was sure a ship was coming, that they were friendly. Pirates lurked out here. It sounded stupid, but wasn't. They were out there.

The waves kicked up a sheet of plastic, clear stuff, looked like a jellyfish. Maple thought it was, but Thirsty knew better, grabbed it, dragged it ashore. He weighed it down with coconuts and driftwood.

"Shelter," he said, while Maple looked on. The thing was heavy-wet, but Thirsty was strong enough to get it where it needed to be.

"It's warm," Maple said. "We have the trees."

"Rain'll come," Thirsty said.

"Pessimist."

"Realist."

The two men shared a stare over the fire, the young know-it-all from San Francisco, and the old salt from nowhere at all.

"Margo's body hadn't washed up," Thirsty said.

"Sharks got her, I'll bet," Maple replied. "You said there were sharks."

"We'd probably see it."

He wondered about that, where her pretty body would turn up. She'd been a real looker, gazelle-quick with puma grace. Big tits with a snaredrum belly, and a little anchor tattoo right above her seashell bikini, in the small of her back. Her laugh was like nothing Thirsty had ever known, a crisp, knowing rat-a-tat-tat that made him blush and stare at his feet and think of waves pounding a shoreline, thankful for his leathertanned face hiding it, but she knew. She knew.

Thirsty and Maple watched the sun set, the sky flashing green just before it went under the horizon.

"We have to keep the fire burning, no matter what," Thirsty said.

"We're going to run out of driftwood," Maple said.

"Least of our worries. If we're not found in a week, we're dead."

"For real? Like dead-dead?"

Maple was as wooden-headed as his name. Thirsty imagined him adrift at sea, floating corklike, clueless. He didn't want to be outlasted by a guy like that. At least Thirst had a little belly fat to tide him over. Maple was a beanpole, and would starve pretty quick when the time came for it.

"Yeah, dead-dead," Thirsty said. "Crab food."

"I eat crabs," Maple said. "Not the other way around."

In the firelight, his young face looked even younger to Thirsty, turning defiance and bravado into petulance and peevishness. He was a kid. Thirsty felt sorry for him.

"Well, then we'd best keep watch," Thirsty said. "If you see a ship, a big one, you shoot off a flare. Up in the air. They're obligated to stop. Doesn't mean they will, but they're obligated to, anyway."

He handed the flare pistol to Maple, who held it with two fingers, like he didn't even want to touch it.

"How about I just wake you up if I see a ship?" Maple asked, handing the pistol back.

"Fine," Thirsty said. He didn't want the kid lighting him up with the thing, anyway. "I'm going to get some sleep. You keep watch—and not just in one direction, either. Look all around. Try not to let the fire get you blind. Just look out to sea. You see something, you tell me."

"Fine, fine," Maple said. "Wake up old man. Got it. Sure has been a trippy trip, dude!"

"Sure has," Thirsty said, finding a place to piss, someplace they wouldn't need later.

As he walked through the shellsand, grateful that he'd been wearing his canvas boat shoes when the boat had sunk, Thirsty thought he heard that song again, along the wind, rolling in the waves and scudding in the surf. It was a pretty song, made him think of Margo, made him a little sad, make him yearn to walk into the water and find the cold water that was down deep, below the sunsoaked surface. It was there, if you went deep enough.

Sometimes, caves sang—water and wind would whistle through blowholes and make lovely, forlorn music, like whalesongs. The song he heard made him think of that, and he just listened to it, while pissing on a palm tree. Fertilizer, he laughed to himself. A few more days and he'd lament pissing away his water. There weren't enough palm trees, not enough coconuts for the both of them. Not for long. A month, maybe? That's if he rationed them, and he could only imagine Maple guzzling coconut milk down, giving himself the shits. Stupid kid.

Thirsty turned his face into the warm wind awhile, listening to the song, until it went away, drowned by the sea breezes that were sending whitecaps their way. Storms would come, but they weren't here yet. It was a good night. Yawning, he made his way back to the fire, which whipped and flicked in the wind. He set a few driftwood chunks on the fire, watched them split and crackle, and curled up by the fire.

He didn't see Maple, but figured he was just walking around. He closed his eyes and dreamed of rum and women.

He woke at sunrise, shivering, chilled, because the fire had burned itself down to a low ebb, just a few coals. The sun was up, and the wind had changed, and Maple wasn't anywhere to be seen.

Thirsty sat up, felt his back creak a bit, tossed some more wood on the fire, stirred up the coals until they glowed an angry orange, and flexed his neck a bit. Sleeping on a beach was nice enough if you just dozed a little, but all night, without proper shelter, not so grand.

He stood up, shook himself out, squinted at the sunrise, scanned the horizon for anything. But nothing was there. He walked toward the water, only to trip on a bottle, half-buried in the sand. Thirsty half-staggered, swung his arms, got his feet under him again, cursed his stubbed toe. The tide was always bringing stuff in. He'd had them make camp above the tidal zone, but this bottle was just past the camp.

Tugging it out, he gasped. Rum. Same bottle from *the Skipjack*. Same damned bottle. Half-full, the way he'd left it. Spiced rum. He dropped it into the sand, looked around.

"Hey, kid," Thirsty yelled. "You been freediving, or what?"

The only answer was the wind, which was no answer at all. He unscrewed the bottle and had a drink, savoring the sweet-hot burn of the rum on his mouth. He thought he'd break into one of those coconuts and pour rum in there, and drink it all down. He'd put the rum in the coconut—that old song came to mind, made him laugh. Fuck the lime, go for the rum.

Thirsty bashed his way into one of the coconuts, and poured several fingers of rum into it, then carefully capped the bottle, laid it down by his feet, and brought the cracked coconut to his lips. Nothing had ever tasted so good. He drank like a marooned pirate, some of it slipping past his mouth and onto his shirt, but he didn't care. He finished and felt his belly get supernova-hot and the beginnings of a buzz already kicking in.

Good kid, getting him that booze. Stupid kid, but a good one.

"Hey, Maple!" Thirsty slurred, stumbling his way along the shore. "Thanks for the rum, buddy."

The waves hit the shore in reply.

"Maple?" Thirsty asked the trees. "Maple? Where you at?"

Thirsty lumbered around the atoll, walked the whole thing, calling Maple's name, but there was no sign. The kid wasn't anywhere. Thirsty walked through the palm grove, calling the kid's name, and he still wasn't there. He simply wasn't there.

"What the hell?" Thirsty said, wiping his mouth with the back of his hand. Had the kid drowned trying to get him his damned rum? He walked back over to where their camp was, took stock of the horizon, gauged where the wreck of *the Skipjack* would be. The tide was up right then, and he was in no condition to swim out there, check things out.

"Maple!" Thirsty yelled, but there was no sign. Then he saw one of the kid's sandals, rolling back and forth in the waves, going up the shore, and then back down, then turning cartwheels when a wave came in. Thirsty went over to it and picked the thing up, looked out to sea, then back up the shore. He saw the other sandal sitting, dry, further up on the beach. He walked over and stared at it, open-mouthed.

The kid's clothes were laid out on the shore, too, wadded up in a pile. He could see where the kid had gone walking, first sandals, then a stagger, then barefoot after he'd kicked off the shoes. The kid had gone crazy, maybe gone on a night swim or something.

Then he saw it, in the sand. Another, smaller set of tracks. A bare foot. A woman's footprint, already half-eaten by the oncoming tide.

Thirsty stared, unbelieving. But there it was, plain as the pink sand between his toes. He just stared and stared, unsure what to do, think, or say. He dropped to his knees by the tracks, and leaned in close, just in case his old, crinkled eyes were playing tricks. But it was there. He stared hard at it, turned his eyes back to the sea. There were no other tracks.

He didn't know how long he'd sat there like a fool, watching the tide drink down the tracks in the sand, wiping everything clean again. Thirsty just turned and took his shoes off, chucked them over his shoulder, and stuck his feet in the water and let the waves wash against his ankles, while he drank, all thoughts of ships and rescue flown like cormorants, far and away from him, a human derelict.

The ocean kept her endless, mindless tidal cycle, the soothing roar of water and the graceful ballet of clouds all in it together, with the Sun as a co-conspirator, embracing the ineffable.

Margo, Thirsty thought. It was the only thing he could think.

The day before the wreck, when they'd gone out to a snorkeling spot, and Maple had thrown himself overboard with a hoot and a holler, Margo had lingered on the boat a bit, finless, not even a snorkel, or a mask. Thirsty hadn't given it much thought at the time, already knee-deep in his first bottle. He just tugged his faded red cap down over his eyes, while Maple splashed and choked on snorkel backwash.

"You going in?" Thirsty asked. Margo smiled at him.

"I'm already there," she said. "I know a great place for diving."

"Oh, yeah? Whereabouts?"

"That way," she said, pointing over his shoulder. Her voice was like clotted cream. Thirsty tipped back his bottle and took a look. He knew this area well enough.

"There's nothing back there," he said. "Just water and shoals and sharks."

"There's a good place," she said. "A special place. Just head thataway. You want Tuvuca to the south/southwest, and Mago to the west. You can't miss it."

"Ain't nothing there, hon," Thirsty said. "I know."

Her eyes were aquamarine that day. They changed with the light. Her bikini was orange and red with white flowers batiked across it. Maple flopped around some more in the water.

"Hey, Margo, come on! It's awesome!" he yelled. She nodded to him, but kept her eye on Thirsty, tucking a wisp of her thick, shiny hair behind her unpierced ear.

"You don't know everything, Skip," she said with a laugh. "Trust me."

"Ain't nothing there," he said. He was Skipper, alright. He knew. Margo walked over to him, moving easily in the bouncing boat, her sea legs smooth and long. She put her hand on his, patting his wrinkled flesh with her long-fingered hands. Her nails looked like abalone.

"I'll show you," she said. "Tomorrow."

Then she laughed, and walked over to the gunwale of the boat and dove easily overboard, making barely a splash as she went in. She swam up to Maple, gave him a playful dunking, which had him coughing and laughing, trying to catch her, but she slipped away from him, even though he was wearing fins. All the while, she watched Thirsty, with that barracuda smile of hers, all teeth.

"Tomorrow, Skip," she said. "I promise."

Thirsty was half-done with the bottle, spite-drinking, at that point. Yeah, she'd showed him something, alright. A tasty little reef, with a taste for boats. He'd run right into it. Not on the charts. How'd she known that? The thought of it made him want to cry, he felt so stupid.

It wasn't possible. She was dead. *The Skipjack* sank like the proverbial stone. Sank like Thirsty's hope for rescue. If he knew where they were, and he didn't know so well by then, being drunk, due east was nothing but Pacific Ocean. Not a damned thing in the world. North (somewhere) was Lomaloma. Northeast, far, far away, was Hawaii. Hell and gone, might as well be Heaven. West was the Koro Sea.

Christ, Thirsty thought. Bearings didn't mean anything if you didn't have a way of getting anywhere. It meant pinning his hopes on tourists, not tradesmen. Tourists. It was like building a boat out of balsa wood. She'd done for them but good.

He finished the bottle, now nicely drunk, and wished he had something to put in the bottle. A message in a bottle, something he'd never done, in all his years at sea. He respected the sea too much to be so stupid. But right now, he wished he could write "Help!" on a scrap of paper and stuff it down in that bottle, and throw it someplace where the current could get it. It hardly mattered.

The rum kept his gut warm, but he'd need to eat again before the day was over. He reluctantly got to his feet, staggered uphill, away from the water, headed for the grove. A special place, alright. He went in amid the palms and sat down in the shade, went to work on a coconut, using a sharp shell to slice the thing open to get at the hard nut inside.

He heard the song, again, stopped what he was doing, took a look. Yeah, he heard it alright. Her song. Pretty, like she was, but edged, like obsidian. He wished he had some of that. Something old, archaic. Something to make into a spear. He meant to do some fishing.

Her song washed in with each crashing wave, and Thirsty gaped, his eyes playing tricks. When you watched the waves, you could see anything you wanted.

"You ain't getting me, hon," Thirsty said.

He'd break that rum bottle, tie it to something. There's your message for you. He thought of the flare gun, in its little box. He got up, went back to the campsite, where the survival kit sat, untouched. The flare gun was in its own little case. He picked up the case and the survival kit and went back to the shade of the grove.

He set the stuff beside him, went back to work on the coconut, muttering drunkenly to himself. He'd go over the litter piles that he'd combed over, see if anything could make a decent spear. He'd kill for some duct tape, but he could tie knots well enough, and figured he could braid off some of that rope he'd found, make his gig out of flotsam and jetsam. Stormalong he wasn't. Captain Nemo, not by a longshot. But he'd be damned if he was going to go the way the kid went, Davy Jones be damned.

While he worked, she sang. He could hear her. Laughing, Thirsty whistled "The Drunken Sailor" to try to drown her out. Her song made him want to swim, to find those bottles of rum in the inky black and drink deep, sharing mermaid's kisses.

Thirsty cracked the coconut and drank the milk, dug out the meat with his thick fingertips. Hard hands, sailor's hands. He belched and then set to work breaking the bottle. It wasn't so easy, breaking a bottle. Not if you wanted it broken right. In movies, they made it look easy, but movies made everything look easy.

He thumped the bottle on a rock, but the thing didn't break, just drove the rock into the sand. Muttering, Thirsty went over to one of the palm trees, and took a swing with it. The first one cracked against the trunk and knocked the bottle from his grasp. Cursing, Thirsty took another swing, and still it didn't break. He looked for a bigger rock, but there really wasn't anything large enough on the atoll.

Looking back at the surf, he thought there might be a rock or two out there. But he didn't want to risk going out there, and cursed himself for being a coward. So he wound up and took a third swing on that tree, giving it everything he had, and the bottle smashed. Too well—the thing broke into jagged shards, one going right up the neck of the bottle and slicing his right hand right open at the palm.

"Fuck!" Thirsty yelled, watching the line of red form on his palm and then become a stream, and then a river, dripping blood on the coral sand. Each flex of his hand widened the cut, increased the flow.

He went to the survival kit and forced it open. A cut was not what he needed right now. Especially one that needed stitches, as this one clearly did. He'd thought his hands were tough, but that bottle had been like a razor. He tore open a pack of iodine with his teeth and poured the stuff on his hand, howling as it shot him through with lightning, the neuronal flash of agony. He imagined that iodine nuking anything living that it came across, a cellular search-and-destroy mission.

After that, he grabbed some gauze and taped it to his palm. Duct tape it wasn't, but medical tape was better than no tape, if he was still able to make some kind of spear. But he couldn't worry about that now. The gauze when from white to pink to red, as he kept direct pressure on it, rooting through the pack for anything else.

He saw a packet of styptic powder, remembered the old styptic pencils he used when he shaved, to stop the bleeding.

He didn't know what styptic meant so much, but figured it had something to do with stopping bleeding. So, he peeled off the gauze, which made his hand bleed all the more, and tore open the packet, then dumped the pinkish powder on his hand.

If the iodine had stung, the styptic powder hurt that much more, and then some. But it stopped the bleeding. Somehow, the crap did it. Relieved, he sat down on the beach, afraid to even move his wounded hand, lest it bleed some more. He just sat there, feeling the pain in his hand along the pink and red line running the length of his palm, wondering what he would do next.

He tried a flex of his fingers, but the needle-pain in his palm discouraged him from moving it. Beyond the shore, she sang to him, a mocking song. Thirsty had almost forgotten about rescue; he just wanted to make his spear.

It was slow going with his injured hand, both from the injury itself, and from how gingerly he handled the broken bottle. He taped the spear to a plastic tube, part of the junk he'd recovered. Then he stuck the thing into the sand, let it catch the light. Clouds laced the sky, but the Sun came out now and then, bathing the atoll with light.

Thirsty felt his stomach growl, and went to one of the cracked coconuts and dragged out some more meat. Even doing that seemed to take more effort. Everything would, so long as his hand was bad. While he sat in the shade and ate, he realized she'd stopped singing.

Her singing was pretty, not like birdsong or whalesong, but something else, like if honey had a sound. Thirsty missed it. He wondered how many boats she'd lured here, how many tourists had died in this place.

She came ashore without a word.

She was radiant and naked, water pearling on her tan skin, tanned in a way that his never would be, her hair curling down her front like a great black snake. Her smile was impossibly wide, radiant in the sunlight.

"Howdy, Margo," Thirsty said. "Lonely, hon?"

Margo looked at the spear, and at Thirsty's hand, her eyes full of mocking sorrow.

"Going fishing, Thirst?"

"Gotta eat something," he said.

She crouched a few feet away from him, the Sun to her back. From where he sat, she was radiant, like the Virgin Mary.

"Nobody's coming," she said. "Not a soul. Nobody comes here, because of the reefs."

"Now you tell me," Thirsty said.

Her face was leonine, round. Childlike, pretty. The eyes were beautiful, but ancient. He hadn't really looked at them before, he realized, hadn't seen what they so clearly showed, now, when they were alone, watching one another, predator and prey.

"Maple walked into the waves willingly," she said. "He's happy, now."

"Not my kind of happiness," Thirsty said. She stood between him and the spear. He had nothing on hand. She was younger and surely quicker than he was.

"You could be happy, too," she said, giving the beach a brush of her perfect toes, her toenails like opals. Margo gave him a sidelong look. "More to the point, you're not going to like being here all alone, dying by inches. That gut of yours won't keep you fed for long, Thirst."

Her own body was both firm and soft at the same time, the wantonness of her nudity like a bludgeon, the boldness of her stance, her fearlessness, frankly intimidating. Thirsty wiped his hands on his salt-crusted shorts, glanced around them. Not a ship to be seen. She'd picked her trap well. He felt stupid.

"I'm offering you a boon," Margo said. "Slow death on this shoal—to call it an island is too generous by half. Or, you can come with me, where it's cool and dark and I'll kiss you and you won't feel pain ever again. Doesn't that sound nice? That rum I left on the shore—yeah, that was me—that was just a little gift for you, a little something to tide you over. There's plenty more beneath the waves. More everything."

Thirsty's tongue felt like sandpaper. "How'd you get Maple to follow you?"

"I just sang," Margo said. "Maple was easy. Didn't even take much of a song, if you really want to know. Sweet boy. All those crabs made him sweet. It's a gesture of my respect for you that I'm even bothering to talk. I don't have to talk, you know."

She hummed a little song, just a little thing from inside her, and it made Thirsty's heart jump, made him break out into a sweat, the beauty of it, prettier than all the Filipinas he'd known, or the Polynesian girls, or the girls from Thailand. A lustrous voice, like finest abalone, it made him want to run his hands all across her. She watched him as she hummed, her eyes hungry and insistent, her mouth mocking. Then she stopped her little song, and Thirsty felt like someone had cut the puppet's strings that held him.

"Christ," he said, shaking.

"He's got nothing to do with it," Margo said. "And he's not going to help you, either. Look, I could just go for a swim, leave you here for a few more days. Maybe a ship would come. Maybe a plane would see you. But it's a big ocean; do you really want to chance it? Things won't be so nice for you in a few more days. This little atoll isn't Bora Bora, now, is it?"

"No," Thirsty admitted. "Never been there, though, so I can't rightly say."

"Too bad," Margo said. "It's an altogether pretty place."

"Pretty as you?" Thirsty asked. Margo indulged him with a smile.

"Well, it's just a place, after all," she said, putting her hands on her lovely hips.

Why didn't she just sing him into the surf? She'd been singing for most of the day. Then it occurred to him: because she couldn't. She was bluffing him. Somehow, he'd been strong enough to resist her. Maybe that rum had been an attempt to soften him up. It had almost worked, too. Thirsty smiled back at her, feeling genuinely good for the first time since the wreck.

"Just the same, it's my place," he said. "I figure I'll stay here for awhile, watch the Sun set. Just sort of take it easy. Fella could get used to a place like this."

He was pleased to see her pout a moment, before she composed herself.

"Alright, Skip," she said. "Enjoy yourself while I'm away."

She turned on her pretty heel and walked back into the waves, her perfect ass swaying almost at eye level with Thirsty as he sat. Knee-deep in the pounding surf, she glanced back at him, her face a mask of momentary menace, before turning away and diving into the next wave, and disappearing.

Thirsty laughed. It felt like a victory, and he savored it: "Bye, hon."

After Margo had gone, Thirsty went to work gathering every bit of driftwood and dry leaves that he could, and stoked the campfire until it got nice and big. Then, he climbed the coconut palms, not caring if he ripped open his cut hand again or not, and knocked loose the coconuts until he had a big pile. Thirsty then ripped off what green leaves he could, and threw them on the bonfire, watching them hiss and spit and throw great puffs of smoke into the sky. Someone had to see. They weren't that far away. So long as the weather held, he'd have some kind of chance.

He'd strip the atoll bare if he had to. Thirsty counted the coconuts. He'd been able to get thirty of them. There were still more on the trees, out of reach. There were a couple of groves across the atoll, on the far side. It wasn't luxurious, but he thought it was doable, at least for one man. The key was to stay optimistic. He remembered reading about that somewhere, how optimists tended to survive in situations like these. Thirsty laughed, feeling stupid, but so long as he breathed, there was hope.

He grabbed his makeshift spear and dared to wade into the water, finding a spot where the waves didn't pound so hard. There were tiny little fish in there, the color of rubies. But small enough to starve a minnow. The real fish would be farther out, past the sandbars, and he didn't dare go out there, in case she was waiting. No, he'd have to content himself with crabs and shellfish. Things up close.

Glancing at his spear, he realized he could string up the remaining shards of glass to catch the light. He'd string them up all over the atoll, in hopes that somebody would see. He'd make it a carnival of light, a regular island jamboree—come to Thirsty's Island Getaway, y'all—bring one, bring all. Bring food, bring ships. Bring rescue. Bring water.

Thirsty whistled while he worked. The bits of broken glass he strung up like Christmas ornaments from Hell, climbing up the palms and snagging fronds and tying the glass shards to them (he'd secured the glass using some of the fishing line he'd found on the beach), so when it was done, they turned and swayed in the breeze, reflecting some light. Maybe not as much as he wanted, but more than there was before.

He set them up around the atoll, and then took a rest, after drinking some coconut milk. It was tough work, climbing trees, and his heart beat hard in his chest. He found a shady spot and sat down heavily, glancing at his handiwork. He could see one of his ornaments flashing a little from across the atoll. It was something. Slender hopes pinned to broken bits of glass—not much to hold onto, but better than nothing. A storm would yank them from the trees, but he had no time for anything else. Who knew when she would come back?

Throwing more wet leaves on the fire, he sent that much more smoke into the sky, a slender white smoke line that looked feeble against the broad blue sky and the endless ocean. He wondered what it would look like, what tourists or tradesmen would think. Pirates? Squatters? Natives? Would they even think it was somebody in need of rescue? And if they did, would they even be able to get there, or would they be too smart to do it—"Hell, no, Boss. That spot of water's full of reefs. We're not going out there."

Though not a prayerful man, Thirsty prayed to the Law of the Sea, that someone would see, and would understand, and would come. And if that prayer was answered, Thirsty thought about what he'd say. He'd tell them the truth they needed to hear—he'd been out in a boat with a shipmate and had caught a reef, sunk, and settled here. He'd not say a damned thing about Margo. For once, a fish story not worth sharing. He'd keep that one to himself, or they'd toss him overboard, thinking him crazy.

He watched a crab watching him, from a safe distance. One of those blue ones, with beady black eyes. Not dead yet, you little fucker, he thought. It opened and closed a claw, slowly. Thirsty kicked sand at it, and it scuttled away.

Thirsty only wanted to get away, to get back aboard a ship again, and to be able to drink rum like a civilized man, in a bar, with the blare of a television and the braying laughter of sailors and Marines and the clueless shambling of tourists and the laughter of pretty girls in brightly-colored dresses with bodies that made him wish he was a younger man. He licked his lips at the thought of it.

And yet, he wondered if he should do something about Margo. It nagged at him, like an itch. The Law of the Sea cut both ways. If a sailor ran into a navigation hazard, he had to chart it, had to warn others, so they didn't run afoul of it. Who knew how many boats Margo had lured out here? He'd kicked himself for not asking her when she'd been around, but he guessed it'd been a lot. He scratched the stubble on his face, his salt-crusted beard. What to do, what to do.

Not one to mull, Thirsty mulled his options, trying to stay optimistic. Save himself. Get the hell out of there. Don't tell his rescuers about Margo. Never come back to that stretch of water again. No "Beware: Mermaid" signs bobbing in the water. He laughed, imagining that sign—green, with a mermaid painted on it.

He could try for another round, come back, try to do something about it. Or he could be that madman at the bar, telling stories about mermaids and cursed shoals. That was something he could do. Try to warn people that way. But then, if he did that, maybe the curious, the bold, and the stupid would try to find this place, try to find her, and she'd get more victims.

Why was it his responsibility, anyway? If somebody was stupid enough to get caught, that's what they got. People like Maple. It was his damned fault Thirsty was there to begin with, by picking Margo up. Partly Thirsty's fault for listening to her great suggestion about a nice stretch of water, but Maple had set it in motion.

Thirsty looked up at the sky, at puffs of clouds that slid inexorably on unseen winds, changing shape slowly but inevitably, mercurial, meteorological. Weather was the ultimate treachery. The sea was a dangerous place. It wasn't his fight. He wasn't supposed to be in this place.

It didn't feel right. He'd go back, somehow get himself another boat. That thought alone made him wince. His insurance would grind his bones into meal over the loss of *the Skipjack*. He'd have to work on other boats to make ends meet. It could take years for him to get his feet back under him. Maybe he'd be able to get some money back, but one look at him and they'd know him for a drinker. His rates would shoot higher than those clouds.

He'd come back, have himself a little fishing trip. He imagined tossing sticks of dynamite into the sea. Thirsty hated the idea of doing that in practice, but the thought of blasting that bitch out of the water made him snicker a bit, a dry, raspy thing that even coconut milk couldn't quite soften.

It was war, simple as that. He'd come back and finish it. She'd taken his boat. That alone demanded payback. Thoughts of revenge didn't stop his stomach from growling, but it satisfied him, nonetheless.

Then he heard a plane flying, a distant drone.

It wasn't much of a plane, which was a good thing. Though Thirsty would've been happy with any plane, he figured a smaller one meant tourists, or somebody local, which might get him help sooner. Maybe best would be an island hopper.

The plane, a Cessna pontoon plane, made its lazy way across the cerulean sky, drinking in the panoramic scene laid out for it, while Thirsty ran up and down the beach, shouting and waving his spear. He threw more greens onto the fire, letting it get big and smoky-fat with fire until the plume was thicker around the middle than he was.

Then he ran and began taking the coconut shells and writing a sloppy SOS in the sand with them, awkwardly, because he was trying to keep his eye on the plane while he did this. He kicked himself for not doing it sooner, but he never was a good planner that way; he was good at reacting to things, versus acting on them. His "SOS" looked like he had a speech impediment, but it would have to do.

The plane, meanwhile, just went its way, dipping its wings and arcing in the inscrutable way planes did at great distances. Then it slowly turned and headed toward Thirsty's atoll, and seemed to take forever to get to it.

Thirsty grabbed his spear, waving it back and forth, hoping to catch somebody's eye. Whether the pilot's or a passenger's, he didn't care.

"Help!" he yelled at the sky, feeling stupid for doing it, but doing it all the same. "Help! Help, you bastards!"

He didn't know how he should gesture, make it plain that he wanted their assistance. The plane, taking forever to arrive, passed by in an eyeblink, roaring overhead, while Thirsty yelled himself hoarse. He'd placed the coconut message on the north side of the atoll, and the plane had arced toward the south.

Had they seen him? He didn't know, but the plane had banked, and was making another pass of the atoll. He imagined tourists with their Nikons, snapping pictures, somebody playing tour guide: "This is an atoll, what happens when an island is close to being reclaimed by the sea. That man on the beach is a squatter. Sometimes people sail out to uninhabited islands and claim them for their own. They're the true beach bums, vagabonds. Down there, you see one waving his spear at us—he's trying to defend his territory from the Shiny Sky Bird that threatens his home."

"Help!" he yelled, moving his arms back and forth overhead in a sort of mayday jumping jack gesture. On this pass, the plane approached with its side to Thirsty's position, and he could see people on board, just shadows, really, ghostly in the Cessna's cabin. Somebody waved to him, a slender pink hand, going back and forth.

Then the plane headed back the way it had come, north by northwest, leaving Thirsty alone and wanting to cry, but unwilling to waste the water on tears.

"Stupid tourists," he grumbled. He hoped the pilot radioed something in. The sea was too choppy to risk landing his plane, he decided, even if the pilot had been inclined to do so. It was easier to just radio something in. He hoped that the pilot did just that. A slender hope, reed-thin, but better than nothing at all.

He watched the plane until he couldn't see it anymore, couldn't hear its drone, and then went about gathering up the coconuts that he hadn't drunk from, yet. In their place, he put whatever litter he could find, hoping the SOS still held up to skyward scrutiny.

Then he sat by his fire and waited for sunset. Somebody would come. It was important to keep some optimism, even through clenched teeth.

He dug coconut meat with his raw fingers, chewed slowly on it, closing his eyes, almost gagging on the taste. Somebody would come. Tomorrow, he'd gather the tiny shellfish, maybe cook them in a coconut shell and pray the thing didn't blow apart.

As the Sun went down, Thirsty realized he didn't remember what day it was, how long he'd been there. It hadn't taken long. Four days? Five? He'd lost count.

"That didn't take long," he said. "My belly's not the only thing full of jelly; I got rice pudding between my ears."

It felt good to hear a voice, even his own. People weren't meant to be alone, not long. And it hadn't even been long. He wondered how inmates bore up under solitary confinement, remembered *The Great Escape*, where the little Scottish guy went crazy, grabbed the electrified fence. Or did they shoot him? He couldn't remember; he just remembered that he went nuts in the Cooler.

The Sun went down and he was alone on the ocean beneath the night's starry sky, beautiful and terrible all at once. It was one thing to snooze in a boat on the sea, but to be on such a tiny bit of land, with such a giant ocean around him, it was too much to bear.

Alone by his bonfire, Thirsty cried.

Somebody would come. Somebody who wasn't her. That night, to the chorus of pounding waves and the restive crackle of his waning fire, Thirsty dreamed of nothing he remembered.

Airlock

WARREN LEFT absolutely nothing to chance. He sat at the command console and waited for his friend Jaro to die.

Thalassonica had been infected by a disease that no one had seen before. A plague that liquefied the victims in days. Warren had seen it and he would not risk the loss of the *Epiphany* to it.

She was a fast, fine ship, with a crew of only 19—as a resupply freighter, her staffing needs were minimal, with robots doing the lion's share of the heavy lifting. They orbited Thalassonica and Warren waited.

"Warren, you ran decontamination," Vina said. "Jaro's clean."

Vina was the Inventory Officer. Warren was Captain. Jaro was Medical Officer. Warren was locked in the Command Bridge. Vina was in the Crew Offload Deck, outside the airlock. Jaro was in the airlock, where he belonged.

"Twenty-four hours," Warren said, glancing at his watch. "Maybe 48. We'll wait up here, see what happens."

"I'm fine, Warren," Jaro said.

"I saw you," Warren replied. Jaro had circulated among the colonists. *Epiphany* had delivered medical supplies to the colony, in hopes of containing the epidemic. But the colonists were all gone.

"Not my fault," Jaro said.

Jaro had snagged his biosuit on a piece of sculpture—a tentacled man wielding a trident. He'd backed away from one of the slithering colonists and speared himself, breaching his suit. Warren thanked his stars that he'd been monitoring it, or Jaro might've snuck back on board, infecting them all.

The victims weren't quite dead. Jaro thought it was a virus that transformed them. He'd bottled one of them. The reddish-pink thing strained against the confines of the bottle. Made Warren sick just looking at it. He didn't want to be a puddle of plasma.

Jaro looked sweaty.

"Maybe it doesn't register on our scans," Warren said.

"I'm thirsty, Warren," Jaro said.

"He should be in Medical," Vina said. "A proper quarantine."

"Airlock's fine," Warren said. He was glad he'd only allowed Jaro to disembark *Epiphany*. It could have been more crew.

Vina glanced at her own watch. "How long has he been in there?"

"18 hours. Not nearly enough."

"We're supposed to disembark in five," Vina said. "Schedules to keep, Warren."

He knew the contract inside and out. Delays were frowned upon, but were understood as being part of business. As Captain, it was his prerogative. Visiting a plague planet made for special circumstances.

"They were waiting for us," Warren said. "They want off."

"They're not sentient," Jaro said. "Not anymore. Pure instinct."

Glancing at Vina on the monitor, Warren knew that plenty of bad behavior could be chalked up to instinct. And he'd thought the things had been stalking Jaro. It was hard to tell from the monitors, but it looked like that to him.

"You should jettison that sample," Warren said.

"We need it," Jaro said. "Somebody has to study this thing."

Warren imagined that thing slipping into a municipal water supply and shivered. No chance. They weren't colonists anymore. They were invaders.

"You didn't put the robots in quarantine," Vina said. "Maybe they stowed away aboard one of them."

Warren had thought about that. The robots were kept in the Cargo Offload Deck, however, and had been sterilized before reboarding. One could use harsher measures with robots: bake the paint right off them and they'd be ready to haul freight the next day. The Tomashi units were built tough.

Jaro and Vina had a relationship. Warren knew this. That's why he'd done things from the command console. It was possible for Vina to override the airlock manually, but Warren had sealed the Crew Offload Deck as a secondary precaution.

Someone was using an arc welder to try to burn into the Command Bridge. Warren had made the access corridor a vacuum, in an effort to seal off the Bridge from invaders. Jaro was a popular crewman; Warren had expected this reaction. He flicked the camera on the corridor and saw three crewmen in spacesuits, the flash of the welder beautiful, mesmerizing, mutinous.

The crewmen were talking to each other: Fossi, Rugo, and Clade. They wanted in badly, to stop Warren from doing what he had to do.

To take his ship from him. To infect everybody.

They wouldn't talk to him. Nobody would listen.

Warren glanced at his watch. He guessed they'd breach the door in maybe ten minutes. *Epiphany* was a solid ship, but her internal hull was softer than her hard outer shell—a curt corporate nod to the crew's needs. He'd ordered the men to back off, but they hadn't listened. Mutiny. The ugliest word Warren knew.

"I'm opening the door," Vina said, pulling the red lever. The airlock hissed open. She and Jaro clasped each other.

"No!" Warren yelled, burying his face in his hands.

He thumbed the external airlock switch, and watched the doomed lovers swim free.

Home Run

"NOW YOU DONE IT, KROG," Evian said. "You done it but good. You gotta go and get it."

Kroger and his crew played stickball in the junk lot outside Mesa Gardens, their neighborhood. Kroger was the best slugger of the polymer baseball that Spiegel had brought from home. It was a blue sphere with a bit of a shine to it, with Ultraball™ laser-stenciled across the face of it, and boy did that thing fly when Kroger hit it. The ball would just flex and spring away from the stick-bat with a crack and go go go past the junkpiles and tires and you'd never see the thing again.

Except, and this was the coolest part, Spiegel had a tracker for his baseball, a pen-shaped little number that tracked the metric distance of the ball in LCD and led you right to it. The ball never got lost, no matter where one hit it. Spiegel was proud as hell of it, and Kroger was proudest that he hit the ball farther than anybody in their group.

"I'll get it, Ev," Kroger said. "I'm not scared."

"Over 66 meters," Spiegel said, whistling.

"Let's just get another ball," Avia said.

"There's no ball like an Ultraball™," Evian said, which was the slogan they used for it on the Toob. "Why'd you aim it over there, Krog?"

The field they used was really more of a slag pit, with piles of gravel here and there, and rats that came out of the drainpipes looking for food or trouble—sometimes when the kids played, they had to use their stick-bat to swing at the rats, get them the hell away from the playing field. The rats were ugly suckers, too, with chemical burns and patchy fur but almost perfect teeth. All of the kids brought their own stick-bats to the game, because you never knew whether rats or gangrapers would be out and about, and it paid to be prepared.

"The wind took it," Kroger said. "Not my fault the wind took it."

"The wind took it," Evian said, spitting at the dusty ground. "You done aimed it there, Stupid."

There were a half-dozen kids per team, with two girls, Avia and Sierra, and the rest boys. Kroger was captain of his team, while Evian was captain of the other team. Everybody came from Mesa Gardens, Evian and his boys from the East Block, while Kroger and his crew came from the West.

"They shoot folks there," Spiegel said. "My dad says so."

Spiegel's dad had a job, which set him apart from most of the other kids. Kroger didn't know where he worked, but knew that they had money, and one day Spiegel and his family would get out of there, and never come back.

Kroger was originally from Texico, so he was used to the sun and the heat when his family moved to Mesa Gardens, looking for work at the Mesa Valley Rock Reclamation Facility, which extracted microelements from otherwise unassuming rock, slag, and gravel. The grinding of the extractors went on day and night, but was really more of a low hum behind the razorwire walls of the plant, because the machines had come from overseas, where things were made a lot better.

A good, tall kid almost drafting age, Kroger had dusty blonde hair and tan skin and smoke-colored eyes, and wanted to be a baseball player. He thought he had the talent to make it work for him, and showed up Evian and his East Blockers whenever he could.

It was that effort that led Kroger to smack that Ultraball™ straight over the wall into Oak Shadows Resort Community. Nobody at Mesa knew what Oak Shadows was like, exactly, because it had a big wall around out made of limestone. And before that wall was a gravel gap and then a tall razorwire fence with "NO TRESPASSING" on it. There were black cameraballs mounted along the walls, and they'd move lazily around, watching folks, red lights blinking. Sometimes Kroger swore those cameras watched them play. They'd joke that the cameras were watching the girls, which made Avia and Sierra laugh nervously and flip the bird at the cameras.

All Kroger knew for sure about Oak Shadows was that it had trees. You could see the tops of the trees past the walls, pretty and green, not withered and brown like Mesa Gardens trees. Those Oak Shadows trees were big and pretty, and had to suck down a lot of water, which meant that Oak Shadows had a lot of money. Big cars came and went from there, but they sped swiftly to the Intrastate 119, escorted by Glox Security vans.

Oak Shadows had some solar power, too. Kroger knew this because his dad had pointed out the collectors that caught the light. When the grid failed and Mesa was bathed in darkness, Oak Shadows blazed away. Sometimes, lying on the roof of their apartment house, Kroger could see the sprinklers spraying lawns over there. Chka-chka-chka they went, and Kroger wanted to run through them.

"We should go to the gate at the front and tell them we lost our ball," Sierra said, tucking her ballcap low down on her eyes. Sierra was sensible, which was why she wouldn't have anything to do with Kroger, who lusted mightily for her, cuz she looked so fine in her Dermaply T-shirts that supported those luscious breasts and gazelle legs she oiled with Evertan™ lotion. Sierra only had ice blue eyes for Evian, which bugged Kroger real bad.

"Yeah, that's real smart," Kroger said. "They'll tell us to shove it."

Spiegel consulted his tracker again. "I can't hardly believe you hit it that far, Krog."

"The wind took it," Evian said.

"Look, I'll jump the fence and go get it," Kroger said. "Up and back in twenty flat."

The kids looked at the fence, then back at Kroger, then started to laugh. Even Spiegel laughed a bit, and it was his damn ball.

"I hit it, I'll git it," Kroger said. "Gimme that tracker, Speeg."

"You gonna throw that over the wall, too?" Sierra asked. "I'm going to the gate to ask them."

"No, wait," Kroger said. "Let me just see if I can find it, first."

Spiegel handed over the tracker, which Kroger hung around his neck, on account of the lanyard that it came with. Kroger wished he could afford an Ultraball™, but his mom said that's the punishment for being poor, like not being able to get stuff.

Kroger patted Spiegel on the shoulder and jammed his ballcap low on his head, squinting in the direction of Oak Shadows. He gave Avia a look, and she returned it. Shorter than Sierra, Avia was broad-hipped and dark-haired, with a slightly toadlike demeanor to her, like buggy eyes and under-slung jaw, but Kroger thought she might be alright. He knew she liked boys lots.

"How long are we gonna wait?" Evian asked.

"Up and back in twenty flat," Kroger said. "Like I said."

"Is that minutes, hours, or days?" Evian asked.

"Seconds, you slot," Kroger said, taking off for the fence. He vaulted up it in a few easy strides, mindful of the razor-wire, which held a few rags and bags, but was pretty clean, compared to the wires Kroger had seen back home.

He wished he'd had some gloves, but did his best to slide under the wire, hoping no cameras were pointing his way. His ballcap snagged in the wire, but he didn't want to waste time fishing it from the fence, so he jumped down to the gravel section between the fence and the wall, liking the feel of the gravel under his shoes, and the crushing sound it made. He thought maybe that gravel had come from the reclamation plant.

Some of kids laughed when they saw he'd lost his hat, but Kroger didn't care. He glanced at the tracker, and saw it gave a bearing for the ball at 30.48 meters SW, the LCD compass tracking the ball faultlessly. Kroger ran up to the wall, which, at this time of day, was well-shadowed. The wall was white limestone shards, jagged.

From this point, he could look out at his friends, who were shading their eyes and looking right at him. Cursing, Kroger waved them away.

"Quit staring at me, Stupids," he said. He didn't want any Gloxmen going after him.

The kids sort of dispersed, milling around this way and that, but keeping their eyes on the action. Kroger didn't know how he could scale the limestone wall, but there was no way he was going to give up with the others looking on.

So Kroger climbed, finding tentative foot- and fingerholds, and slowly made his way up the wall, reaching the top after a few missteps and falls. At the top was a monofilament line. Kroger knew this because he could see it catch the sunlight, like a lengthy bit of rainbow stretching out along the wall. He'd seen some monofilaments before on the Toob.

The filament posed a problem, because Kroger was afraid he'd lop off his fingers on it. He couldn't imagine how much money it had cost Oak Shadows to string a line like that along the whole compound, but he figured it was a whole lot.

He stepped up onto the wall, peered in, and was amazed at all the green. Turning back to gaze at his friends, he saw only brown, white, yellow, and red. The green was prettier. Kroger gave them a jaunty wave, and then jumped over the wall.

Inside the walls of Oak Shadows, even the air was sweet. There were tall trees and winding hills covered in green, and a lake and a fountain. And the houses were big and white. Maybe they all looked the same, but they weren't covered in tinfoil and plastic, with polywood hammered over holes in the walls. The houses were the most amazing thing Kroger had ever seen. He almost forgot the Ultraball™.

But, looking at Spiegel's tracker, he saw it was 28.95 meters S/SW. So, Kroger ran close to the wall, like a rat, and worked his way from tree to tree, seeing the Ultraball™ laying half in the Sun and shadow like a giant blueberry that had fallen from one of the giant trees.

Kroger checked the tracker, and confirmed that this was Spiegel's ball. Then he cocked his arm back and chucked the thing back over the wall, hoping it would get where it needed to be. If not, he could get it once he went back over. He checked the tracker, to see how good his throw was: 32.9 meters. That might be over the wall. He hadn't noticed when Spiegel had first taken his reading. He'd assumed it was from the plate. Baseball was a game of centimeters, after all. He stuffed the tracker into his pocket, marveling at the wonder that was the Ultraball™.

The splashing of the fountain and the birdsongs he heard made him want to stay awhile. Oak Shadows was a neighborhood, just like his, except everything was better. Every single thing. There were flowers, and gardens, and paths and so many trees. It was quiet, too. He thought maybe he'd steal a flower and give it to Avia, and boy would that make Sierra jealous. And maybe Evian wouldn't look so sweet to her.

He heard laughter, and saw some kids riding across a trail in a little cart that whirred quietly as it went. A boy and a girl, clean and dainty, protected from the Sun by a bubble that covered the cart. They didn't see him, since he was concealed by some flower bushes he couldn't name.

The cart had to be electric; Kroger had heard about them, though all they had in Mesa Gardens were corn-fed go-karts that ran on vegetable oil and farted their way up the street. They would throw rocks at those fart-kart kids. This Oak Shadows cart was white and polished, with that lightly tinted bubble and the laughing kids inside. Kroger wanted to steal that cart and take it for a spin with Avia, but he knew he'd lingered too long, and went to get out of there.

He was even more aware of the need to flee when he heard the click of a gun's hammer and saw a Glox Security Man standing there with a 10 mm Sapu-Kinjen semiautomatic pistol pointed at his face.

Kroger knew Glox by name because they had billboards everywhere and ads on the Toob. Their maroon uniforms were unmistakable, as were their patented six-pointed star badges that looked like two crescents crisscrossing, one silver, and the other gold.

This Gloxman's badge was stamped with 139 on it. The guy looked a few years older than Kroger, and a lot stronger, and for a second, Kroger thought about running anyway, but the guy kept the gun leveled on his chest.

"Don't do it," he said, reaching for his Quickphone. "Biff, this is Wallace. I got the perp. Bring the truck."

Something squawked back from the Quickphone, but it was a series of numbers, and Kroger didn't know what they meant.

"Mister, I was just getting my ball," he said.

"Save it," the man said, his face freckled, his hair a bright red, shaved close to his head. "We're going to wait for Biff. What's your name?"

"Kroger," he said. The man grimaced like Krog had said a bad word.

"Mesa kid, hmm? You got a first name, or is that your first name? Your mom a whore?"

Kroger wanted to deck the guy right there for insulting his mom. He knew plenty of kids whose moms were, but his mom wasn't. Wallace the Gloxman's eyes never wavered from Kroger's face.

"It's just a name," Kroger said. "Last name's Ward. Why? Am I under arrest?"

"Can you read? Do you know what 'No Trespassing' means?"

"I was looking for my ball," Kroger said.

"Shouldn't be hitting them into people's yards. Suppose you broke a window with that crappy ball of yours," Wallace said. "This is private property. You know what *that* means?"

Kroger was feeling a bit insolent, layered someplace under the fear. "It means 'no trespassing.' Look, I wasn't gonna steal nothing."

Wallace nodded. "Damn right you weren't, Hillrat. The people who live in Oak Shadows expect a certain level of privacy to their homeowning experience. They've got their own kids, their own families, their own lives. They don't want rats like you creeping over their walls. You saw that monoline, didn't you? Anything bigger than a squirrel goes over that line, we know where it is. We saw you the moment you got stupid and went where you weren't supposed to. Private property means 'stay the hell out.'"

"I was leaving, man," Kroger said. "Let me just go, how about?"

Wallace shook his head. "I'm paid to keep this little community trash-free. You might say I'm a custodian of sorts. You see any trash around here? Besides you, I mean?"

"I ain't trash," Kroger said, looking around, and had to admit that it was very clean. Not a weed to be seen on the emerald grass. The cart with the kids was nowhere in sight. Even the air smelled sweeter than in Mesa.

"Do you know what 'initiation of force' is, Kroger?" Wallace asked. "That's when one party injures another. When you went over that wall, you *invaded* Oak Shadows. That's what you are. An invader. There's a lot of rich people behind these walls. They pay big money for protection, to feel safe. For their property to be protected. They pay big money to avoid hillrats like yourself. Now, if I let you go, maybe you'd be smart and stay gone. You look about ready for the Service, so maybe you'd be gone. Or, maybe you'd be stupid and come back. Maybe you'd try spray-painting some stupid little picture on our clean walls. Did you notice any crap on those walls you climbed? No? That's because of the work we do. Peace of mind. That's what we offer. In a minute, a little truck is going to come up, and you're going to get in, and we're going to drive off and get you back where you belong."

"All my friends saw me go over the wall. They know I'm here."

"Mesa Gardens hillrats," Wallace said. "You think we care about what some hillrats have to say? You think *anybody* does?"

Kroger began to sweat, despite being sheltered beneath the shadow of one of the many beautiful trees. He saw the truck come up, marked with the distinctive Glox Security seal, with "Peace of Mind" written on the side. Maroon and white.

"Where am I going?" Kroger asked, as a burly bald man got out and opened the doors of the truck. He carried a stun baton in his meaty hand-slab. Wallace gestured with the pistol.

"Just get in the van," he said. "And we'll pretend this never happened."

Kroger got in the van, afraid of being shot in the back while trying to run. The van drove off, Kroger stewing in the dark. He tried the doors, but they didn't open from the inside. He hoped they didn't take him to the cops, because cops were total gangsters, and his mom didn't have enough money to pay to get him back. He edged his way to the front, where a dark window was. He could see the guys beyond it.

"I live in Mesa Gardens," he said. "It's down the street from your place."

The guys didn't answer, and the truck kept going. And going.

"Mesa Gardens," Kroger said, taking out the tracker and noting that it was still registering the Ultraball™: 8 kilometers N/NW. 11.2 kilometers. 14.48 kilometers. 16.8 kilometers. How was anybody supposed to hit a ball that far?

"You guys passed my place," Kroger yelled, banging on the window. He looked at the gauge. 20.9 kilometers N/NW. He didn't know where that was.

The truck stopped, and the Gloxman opened the door.

"Get out, Hillrat," he said, not waiting for a response, but grabbing Kroger and yanking him out of the back of the vehicle. Kroger didn't know where the hell he was, beyond being 20.9 km N/NW of where he had been. They'd taken him to the desert. There was nothing around them but hills and arid scrubweed.

The Gloxman shut the door. "This is the natural habitat for a hillrat, don't you think?"

Then he took out a stun gun and shot Kroger full of voltage that dropped him to the ground. The guy worked Kroger over three times with the stun gun, making Kroger writhe and wail each time. Then he holstered the thing and walked away.

"Have a nice walk home, Hillrat. Don't let me ever see you in Oak Shadows again."

The men were laughing, and drove off, leaving Kroger twitching in the weeds, with only dust and scorpions for company. It took awhile for the stun gun to wear off, for life to come back to his limbs. Kroger sat up eventually, cursing the Gloxmen, cursing his thirst, cursing life, and cursing Oak Shadows worst of all.

Taking out the tracker, Kroger started the long walk home, heading south by southwest. It'd take him at least three hours to get home, he estimated. Home looked very far away, shimmering in the heat. His folks were gonna kill him. He'd tell them he was practicing for Army survival training. Maybe that would keep them off his back, when he turned up hours later, dusty and dehydrated.

Survival training. When he got back to Mesa, he'd give Spiegel back his tracker, and would borrow that polymer bat of his. Then he'd stalk Oak Shadows, wait for that Gloxman to drive home to wherever it was he lived. And then Kroger would show him just how much of a slugger he really was.

///

Hours after Kroger's abduction, one of the Oak Shadows Land Management workers, a fella from Texico named Maaco Janssen, saw something flapping in the razorwire while he was driving a cart over the gravel midway between the security fence and the protective wall. He parked his cart and climbed atop the cab, reaching for the thing, which turned out to be a ballcap for the Texico Tigers, nicely worn, a bit weathered, caught on the wire.

He snagged the cap carefully, looked it over, tried it on. It was a bit small, but he thought it'd be just right for his kid. He pocketed the cap and got back to work, raking rocks for Oak Shadows.

The Shape

THE SHAPE could tell it was time to go from the weeping of
the woman, the half-pretty bottled blonde with mascara running down her tear-chapped cheeks, her face split wide in
a rictus of grief racked by spasms of shoulder-heaving, air-
gulping sobs.

Half-pretty was enough to draw the eye but not force it to
memorably linger. That's what had first drawn the Shape to
her, when it had looked for another disguise. Beauty was a
currency recognized in all countries, something the Shape
found more valuable than any fickle means of monetary
exchange.

It had picked her up along the way, spent some time with
her in the guise of Ernest Caruthers, the last hominid it had
assumed. It had thought that the man's genial, comparatively
benign demeanor would offer a suitable cover for its operations, but, faced with the woman whose sobs were painful to
the Shape's ears, it realized that Ernest's time was passing.

"I'm sorry, honey," it said, using Caruthers's folksy tenor
voice to create an impression of intimacy. "This just isn't going to work out."

"You've ruined me," the woman said.

"No, no, no," the Shape said. "I just can't take you with me,
is all."

The woman wiped her eyes with a backhanded swipe,
smearing the mascara.

"But you promised."

"I know," it said. "But promises are made to be broken. I can't take you."

Her name was Celeste. The Shape liked that name. It made it think of home.

"If it's any consolation," it said. "Part of you will always be with me."

Celeste just sobbed. "I need you. Don't you have any idea?"

The Shape understood this. The unity it could bring a person, if it so chose, was a more compelling sensation than anything the hominids could experience on their lonely world. It should not have led the woman on, letting her sample its forbidden fruit, the nectar that it yielded—far stronger than any clumsily distilled narcotic.

"If you go, I'll tell," Celeste said.

Slyly, the Shape reached out and touched her chin, bringing her wavering, watery gaze into its own. It still spoke as Caruthers.

"No one would believe you," it said.

"I will fucking die without you."

"I don't want you to die," it said. "You won't die, if you do as I ask."

The Shape was pleased to see hope kindled in her eyes, laced with urgent need. The strength of her conviction, whether buoyed by sincerity or addiction, didn't truly matter to the Shape. What mattered was its assignment.

"Anything," she said. "Oh God, anything."

"I'm a spy," it told Celeste. It had used her to get at Trinity Savings Bank in Philadelphia, where she'd worked as an accounts officer. It had approached her as Caruthers, looking to open a bank account.

She'd been eager, then, her hair conservatively trussed with clips and her banker's blouse of ivory silk with her gray wool skirt and shiny black pumps. Tortoise-shell glasses gave her a pleasantly professional silhouette that the Shape almost immediately had thought would be useful.

It was what compelled the Shape to ask her out while finalizing the account business. Of course, it declined to open an account, making it up to her over lunch, playing coy, pretending to be interested in the mechanics of variable interest rates.

"A spy?" she'd asked. "For who?"

"Nobody you'd know," it said. "I answer to a higher power."

"Are you an angel?" she asked.

The Shape smiled at the quaint thought. It had studied the culture well enough to know about the obsession with the winged, quasi-benevolent parahominids that represented native mysticism and appeared to satisfy latent psychosociocultural needs.

"Do you think I am?"

"I think you're a devil," she said, wiping her hands on her jeans.

"Same thing, really," the Shape said. It didn't much relish philosophical discussion with hominids, whose brains tended toward a simple duality—good and bad, right and wrong, white and black, strong and weak, true and false. Almost every hominid problem could be structured in that way, with a few, marginally more enlightened members of the species taking a middle ground between those two points, preferring a shade of gray. Gray was a color the Shape was far more familiar with, as its people had long ago abandoned more elaborate coloration for the manifold flexibility of gray. Flexibility and adaptability was the defining characteristic of the Shape's people.

It had put those qualities to great use in its assignment, gathering information and performing missions of sabotage, larceny, and assassination that were required of it by its superiors. The robberies were simply a means to a larger end, assignments not entirely worthy of the Shape's expertise, but obviously part of a grander design that the Shape was not privy to.

In Philadelphia, after leaving Celeste in a metanarcotic stupor, it had assumed her identity. This was neither a slow nor a difficult process for the Shape, as it was a quality possessed by all of its people, as easy as breathing. It merely involved the contraction of external morphophores that allowed the Shape's epidermis and skeletal structure alter to accommodate the desired DNA sample, which it kept inside, along with all of the samples it had acquired in its time on Earth.

The Shape was alien through and through; the transformation was purely cosmetic—the Shape's people dealt with surfaces, not depths. They could not radically alter their internal structure, nor did they wish to. If a hominid doctor had bothered to put one of his diagnostic tools to the Shape's chest, he would have immediately realized it was not a human being standing in front of him. Of course, had he done that, he would have been dead. The Shape did not allow its identity to be compromised.

Fortunately, the Shape found that most people did not have any reason to suspect an impostor, and treated pretty much everyone they met as who they actually were, and with the right application of breezy conversation and flippant observations, the Shape could pass as just about anyone, at least superficially.

For longer-term assignments that required actual penetration of a facility and full assumption of an identity, the Shape had to use more rigorous means, involving intense surveillance of a target for assumption, learning routines, friends, family, lovers, tics, foibles, preferences, prejudices. All such things. But for the Shape, able to alter its appearance at will, it was easy to tail and shadow a target. Operations like that were for high-priority targets, and were undertaken with a full support staff, rather than with a lone field agent.

Entering the Trinity Savings Bank, and, using Celeste's nectar-fueled knowledge of the bank, the Shape breached the vault and left with over $800,000 in cash without a shot being fired. It had simply walked out with the money in a gym bag that it had loaded into a traveling suitcase, which it had been careful to roll in, telling any coworkers who asked that it was going on a trip. It had gotten Celeste to take the week off as a vacation as a cover story.

The only flaw in its disguise had been her hair. As it had adopted her form, based on her DNA, it had her natural hair color, which was a light brown, instead of the blonde she had used. A few people had noticed, coworkers of hers.

"Celeste, did you dye your hair?" a female coworker asked. Her nametag said her name was Luz.

"Yes," the Shape answered. "Do you like it?"

"Sure. Where are you going?"

"New York City," the Shape replied.

"Fun," Luz said.

"I hope so," the Shape said. "Well, I'd better be going."

And out the door it went. Nobody had reason to suspect her, because Brinkman had a solid five-year work record there, always favorably reviewed. And she had informed the Shape of what security measures there were at the Trinity Bank.

The stolen money was then put to profitable use, all part of the assignment. The Shape took one-tenth for itself, and then funneled the remainder to various enterprises that served its people, to no less than six front businesses that were run by other Shapes in Philadelphia (a liquor store, a church, a bar, a grocery, a restaurant, and a book publisher). It spent part of the day making the cash drops to its confederates. The Shape didn't question why the money was needed; that was not its job. Its job was simply to acquire it.

The Shapes knew each other by touch, and yet, in case anyone was watching, they kept up the pretext of their disguises. Making its last drop, the Shape went to the book publisher (Celestial Books), which sold evangelical textbooks to willing markets, mostly in the South. Its pickup person was Mr. Ezekiel Lee, who was another Shape.

"Good morning, Mr. Lee," the Shape said.

"Good morning," Lee said. Lee looked uneasy. "Do I know you?"

"Celeste Brinkman," the Shape said, holding out its hand. They shook hands, exchanging polypeptides and recognizing each for what the other was. "I have a package for you."

Without waiting for a response, the Shape took out a bag that held several boxes of bundled cash. Lee took it, placing it below the counter.

"You're very kind to deliver it to us directly," Lee said.

"Kindness has nothing to do with it," the Shape replied. It was their code phrase, to confirm receipt of the purloined currency. Lee pulled a small package from behind the counter.

"Would you be so kind as to mail this for me, my dear?"

The package was a brown-wrapped box. The code phrase meant that the Shape was to take it and open it in a secure area; it likely contained its next assignment.

"I would be delighted," the Shape replied, again in code, confirming receipt of its next assignment. "Goodbye."

"Bye, now," Lee said, waving as the Shape left Celestial Books. They would not meet again.

The Shape had dropped the package onto a desk when it got back to its hotel room, where Celeste was gradually coming out of her euphoria. The Shape quickly undressed and took a shower, assuming the form of Caruthers as it did. It came out of the shower wrapped in a towel. Despite the arsenic in the water, it felt clean.

Of course, when Celeste sobered up, she was terrified to see her own face plastered on the evening news, wanted for her brazen theft that she did not actually commit, and, in truth, could not verifiably say that she did not commit, owing to her intoxication. Though this disbelief on her part was explained when she came to learn more about the Shape's nature.

"What the hell is with my hair?" she asked. "It looks brown. That wasn't me."

"You're right, honey," the Shape said, looking into the package it had carelessly left on the table. Not that it would have mattered if Celeste had looked at it, because it wasn't in her language. The message said:

WE'RE ONTO YOU.

It was in the Shape's language. Inside the package was a key for the Lucky Save Cash Store, NYC, Box Number 1037. This was stamped on the stumpy bit of brass. The Shape pocketed the key and immediately tossed the package and the message into the trash, after noting where it had been postmarked. Philadelphia.

"Pack up," it said. "We're leaving."

It went to the window and peeked out. It had to make a trip to Celestial Books, see what had happened, exactly. Ezekiel Lee was a Shape, so the nature of the message was uncertain. The Shape had to assume that Lee knew the contents of the envelope.

"Mistaken identity," Celeste said. "I've got to call the police."

She went to the phone, but the Shape stopped her, holding down the phone. "They think it's you, honey. You go to the cops, and it'll be bad for you."

The Trinity Bank heist had been a high-profile crime, as the Shape had intended, wanting the spotlight to be squarely on Ms. Brinkman, and not on itself. That was part of the reason behind its recruitment of her. A spy knew how best to use the native assets at its disposal. That was why the message was so disconcerting. Who was onto it?

After the big robbery, it knew that it would have to dispose of Celeste sooner than later, which was how it came up with the job it intended for Celeste herself.

"But I didn't do it," Celeste said, crying. She touched her hair. "Look!"

"I know," the Shape said. "But they'll just think you bleached it."

"Of course I bleached it," Celeste said. "This is my normal hair color. I mean, not natural, but normal. That brunette, I don't know who the hell she is. She looks sort of like me, I guess. It's hard to tell on those security cameras."

The news show displayed Celeste's work ID photograph. She wailed when she saw it, again trying for the phone, which the Shape kept from her.

"We've got to get out of town," it said. "New York, howsabout?"

"New York? I'll be busted for sure," she said. "I'll just tell them I didn't do it."

"They won't believe you," the Shape said.

Her eyes were wild, searching around the room. "If I stole it, where's the goddamned money?"

The Shape pointed to a bag that sat on the table. Its cut. Celeste ran over to it, tore open the bag with shaking hands, yelping as bundled bills spilled out.

"I didn't do this!" she said. "I've been framed. Besides, it's not all here. No way is that $800,000."

Then she turned and stared hard at the Shape, as if she'd seen it for the first time. "You did it."

"Me? I'm a fella, honey," it said, glancing at its watch. What had happened? Who was onto it?

"You did it," she repeated. "I don't know how, but you did."

The Shape didn't care if she went to the police. They would not believe her. It said as much to her, as she began to sweat. Withdrawal from the nectar came quickly, and would begin to erode the clarity of her thoughts. In such a state, she could be persuaded.

"You did it," the Shape said. "As far as anyone knows, you did it."

She ran out the door, and the Shape didn't stop her. It just pocketed the money and checked out of the hotel room, packed the car, and waited in the parking lot, wondering if it was under surveillance even then. It scanned the near-empty lot, which contained some old-model hominid cars and a motorcycle. Nothing out of the ordinary.

The Shape drove off, heading to Celestial Books, keeping its eyes on the road, both in front and behind it. It could not spot any tails.

When it reached Celestial Books, it found the warehouse to be closed. Boarded up, as if it had never been in business. It glanced at its watch. It had only been there about five hours before. It took out a phone and called the Station Chief. The line was busy. The Shape hung up without a moment's hesitation.

Had its station been compromised? It didn't seem possible. And yet, the storefront was there, unused and abandoned. The Shape wanted to slip inside, to see what it could find, but was worried that it was, perhaps, a trap. Then again, Lee could have trapped it when it had showed up for the drop-off. It decided to return to the hotel.

In the parking lot, Celeste showed up again, sheered in sweat, shivering.

"You've ruined me," she said. She looked like walking death. The Shape smiled, its teeth almost bluish-white.

"Ready to go to New York City, honey?" it asked.

"Fine," Celeste said. "Wherever."

She got into the car and huddled by the door. The Shape rewarded her with an amber kiss that made the shakes go away.

The drive to New York City was unnervingly uneventful, with the Shape minding the road and everything upon it, trying a couple of more calls to its station, continuing to get busy signals. At that point, it was certain that, somehow, there had been a breach in the operation. This made Lee's actions all the more perplexing, since Lee was a Shape.

Shapes had become double agents before. It was not unheard of. But no Shape had done so on this assignment. The very idea of it was absurd—there was nothing the locals had that Shapes would possibly need badly enough, no enticement or inducement that could persuade a Shape to act against its own people in that way.

And yet, if it had intended to catch the Shape unawares, it should not have delivered the warning message. Unless that was part of the operation. The Shape was aware enough of psychological operations to know what kind of cranial havoc they could wreak. Yet even the translation of a message pointed to a compromised Shape, for the hominids could not have broken the language on their own.

It had been expecting another assignment after successful completion of the robbery. Now, without that, it realized it was a free agent. It didn't have to go anywhere it didn't want to go. It thought about this as it fingered the key in its pocket. And yet, the Shape wanted to see what the next move of its unseen adversary was. It could not otherwise rest.

The Shape laid the stolen money out onto the bed. It placed no honest value on such things, but recognized the utility of it when dealing with humans, and had hoped its initiative had paid off with the Section Head. Now, with the station apparently compromised, such initiative could not be rewarded.

Celeste laid beside the cash, her face sweaty and her lips trembling.

Upon many of the bundled dollars was the genetic residue of many thousands of hominids. The Shape ran its hands over the bills, taking that varied information in. So many types, so many individuals. An endless parade of identities to assume.

It looked up at her, still wearing Caruthers' homespun smile.

"You wantin' another taste, darlin'?"

Celeste's jackal eyes narrowed, she licked her lips, faced Caruthers on her knees, atop the bed, wiping her sweaty hands on her thighs.

The Shape was momentarily unsure how much of the nectar to give. It knelt onto the bed and leaned in toward the woman, whose mouth opened wide, moaning as she did so, in anticipation of her reward.

Of course, it would have been easier—kinder—to simply kill her. The Shape understood this. It had certainly done as much (and worse) in other assignments. But it was chagrined to note that it had become grudgingly fond of the hominids, because of having to occupy their world for so long. It did not want to kill more than it had to. It was a professional.

It leaned in close and kissed Celeste, long and hard upon her quavering lips. It could feel her flesh shudder within her slender frame, for the nectar fed her better than anything she could find in her own world, and she had thinned out while staying with the Shape, subsisting almost entirely on a diet of the venom.

A dose of nectar brought bliss, two doses brought ecstasy, three brought unconsciousness, and four brought the most delightful death a person could know.

As they kissed, it made its venom glands contract, sending a drop of the amber nectar to its lips, which it shared with Celeste, who brought her arms up and around its neck, latching on for every drop of it, sweeter than honey, stronger than heroin. The Shape let her tongue slap greedily inside its mouth, seeking every drop of it.

It pushed her back onto the bed, where she writhed, grunting with delight.

"Good Christ," she murmured. "I don't even care where you come from. Just give me MORE!!"

The Shape had strung her along for days that way. The hominid system was barely able to process the neurotoxin, a happy accident of biochemistry, for a fuller metabolizing of it would have led to immediate death. That was the function of the nectar. It was a defensive thing, and only through much trial and error did the Shapes realize it could have another function.

"More," the woman said. The Shape obliged, leaning over her, holding a drop of the venom on its lips, letting it drop, honeylike, into her waiting mouth, where she gurgled with delight on the alien ambrosia, gasping and gaping, eyes glazed.

The Shape went to take a shower, cleaning the alien filth from its skin. It hated the dirty world it had been assigned, even as it enjoyed the work itself. The hominids did not take care of their world, or of themselves. Their cells sang a discordant song, packed with pollutants and preservatives that came from all across the globe, slurring their cellular speech and syncopating their biorhythms. The Shape had far greater control over its own body, and was all too aware of the industrial pollutants that entered it with each intaken breath. It expelled them with prejudice. It could not wait for the day when it could leave this place forever, for a better assignment.

And now that hope was dashed. The station had been breached. Immediate reassignment was in order, and yet, the Shape did not want to go to the rendezvous area, for who could be sure that this was secure? Once one part of the network had been compromised, it was reasonable to assume that all of it had. The Shape could only imagine what the other field agents had done, or whether they had even become aware of the breach.

Celeste came to the door, opening it, barely visible in the gusts of steam the Shape made from its shower. She staggered over to the shower stall, pressing herself against the glass, naked and sweating, her eyes like bruises, half-lidded, her hair a mess, her grin leaching into a leer as she slid against the shower glass with a fleshy squeak. Several of the hominid dollars stuck to her body, like leaves on the bottom of a well-worn shoe.

"More," she moaned.

"You've had enough," the Shape said. "Aren't you high enough already?"

"More," Celeste said. "God, please, more."

The Shape wanted her to go to the Lucky Save Cash Store and check on Box 1037. That was to be her assignment, to see what the enemy had waiting for the Shape there. If she was intoxicated, she would be unable to carry out the task. Then again, the Shape thought it could simply wait until she sobered up, and then have her visit the place. But the Shape didn't want to wait around, ceding initiative to the adversary.

Grudgingly, the Shape obliged her, leaning out the door, giving her a third dose from its lips. She slid down the side of the shower stall, where she drooled and dozed, while the Shape finished its shower.

It toweled off and got dressed, and then took most of the money from atop the bed, which it put in its pockets in carefully banded bundles. Then it went back into the bathroom and picked Celeste up, where she muttered in her sleep, a sugary smile upon her lips.

Almost tenderly, the Shape tucked her into bed, giving her a kiss atop her sweaty forehead, turned out the lights, let her sleep on her bed of stolen cash—some $5,000 in all. She'd sleep for perhaps 16 hours, if left undisturbed. The Shape walked out of her life at exactly 8:35 p.m., and into the infernal stink of the city.

The Shape cased the Lucky Save Cash Store, assuming the guise of a Korean woman, middle-aged, with graying hair and a steady, rolling gait. It left the car in a parking deck and walked four blocks to pass the Cash Store three times. It was not worried about forensic evidence left in the car, since it would show up as Caruthers and Celeste.

The Lucky Save Cash Store was a dismal little block of a building, with a worn yellow awning stretched tight across dented aluminum tubing. The front window appeared to be Lexan, at least an inch thick, with "Lucky Save Cash Store" painted across the front, along with a phone number. The Shape noted the number, taking advantage of its people's facility with numbers to recall it later, when it needed to.

The interior of the place was leprous floor tile, a tiny brown countertop with some scattered pens, and across from it, a row of old, brassy safety deposit boxes. The back of the place was partitioned by a heavy wall that had two "teller" windows in it. There was a security door on the left-hand side.

Passing by the store a final time, the Shape walked around the block, looking for an alley entrance. It found one on the other side, a litter-spattered zigzag of brick and asphalt piled with plastic bags of trash and overturned cans, where a lonely, sickly tree squatted, clawing vainly skyward for a hint of fresh air and rain, its trunk wrapped in a rusting wrought iron skirt.

The Shape made its way through the alley, mindful of the rats that first watched it, then fled from it, their twitching rodent noses seeming to sense something out of place with the Shape. Animals were always problematic; one could never know how they would react.

A gray steel door marked "LSCS" and "1037" on it indicated where the Shape was to go. It had thought the key was to a safety deposit box. Perhaps it was. It slid the key into the lock, and was pleased to find that it turned.

Looking to the left and to the right, the Shape opened the door. Then everything exploded in a flash of white phosphorous, igniting the Shape, the steel of the door, the plastic alley bags, some of the rats that had lingered, watching. Even the brick caught fire.

//

The phone rang in the Shape's room. Celeste picked up, setting her antivenin kit on the nightstand. She held a syringe in shaky hands, the needle thick to her watery eyes, full of milky liquid. She held a small round mirror to her face, the edges of it distorting her reflection. She stuck her tongue out at herself.

"Yeah?" she said into the phone, not knowing who to expect on the other line.

"Hello, Clover. This is Stinger." The call sign was correct, but the Shape could have known that.

"Yeah?"

"Nice job," Stinger said. "It's done."

"About fucking time," she said. Then she hung up, sticking the needle underneath her tongue and pushing the plunger.

Vacancy

SOMETIMES MEGHAN felt like she didn't even exist.

It was the nature of her day, from her morning routine, to her daily commute downtown, to jostling for coffee at Café Vostok, to entering the lobby of the Tritanium Building, to the rows of elevators alternately gobbling people up and expelling them, to the floor of her workplace, the cubicle cemetery where she held a plot for the last decade, watching her black hair give way to white, until she had the start of a stripe like a skunk. It was, perhaps, the most noteworthy thing about her.

She'd do her job without distinction either way—it used to be that doing a good job was something to be rewarded; today, it was just a formality, unworthy of recognition. And she did feel unrecognized.

Meghan didn't just feel marginalized: Meghan felt dead. But not one of the honored and honorable dead; she felt like a Jane Doe in her own life, an unmarked grave.

She told her friend, Jon, about it. They would sometimes ride the El together, the Brown Line. She told him on the way home, as the train wound its way north.

"We're all invisible," she said. "Anonymity is one of the survival mechanisms of urban living, I think."

The train car was packed, everybody busy doing nothing, just standing there. A few were reading, most were staring out the window, others were texting or playing games on their phones, others just staring halfway blankly at nothing.

"I guess so," he said. Jon worked in the Marketing department, and though he was losing his hair, Meghan found him attractive—baldness became him, somehow. He would shave his hair down, rather than pretending he wasn't going bald, rather than getting plugs or implants.

Jon was always at the gym, kept himself pretty fit. She didn't want to think about whether he was older or younger than she was; it was too painful a line of thought to pursue. She guessed younger, because she was older than most of the people in her department. That kind of thing happened when you stayed at a job too long.

She'd worked at Paramort Publishing, had seen her peers come and go, while she had remained. She hadn't planned on it; it just happened.

Things just happened to Meghan.

Jon just happened to her.

She thought maybe he liked her, but sometimes she thought maybe he was gay.

He was ambiguously manly, and his aloof affability contributed to those suspicions. That, and he'd never asked her out, even though they'd worked together for the last three years.

"I'm just saying, look around you," she said. "We're all just going through the motions. Everybody does it."

Jon glanced around them, his tea-colored gaze sphinxlike to Meghan's own pale blue eyes. "It's rude to stare, so nobody does it. It's a matter of etiquette."

"You know some of them are totally listening to us," Meghan said. "They're just pretending not to."

She imitated one of the commuters, a lanky young man in a gray pinstriped suit with a pink shirt underneath, his hair a spray of brown, gelled up into a frozen wave.

Meghan peered out the window, gazing at the downtown skyline, her face blank. She could hear Jon chuckling, was pleased by that.

Then Meghan saw *it*.

The train was paused on the track, waiting for some other train ahead of them to advance. This was what the driver said.

But she saw it: The most beautiful building ever.

It was a greenish-silver spire, circular, cylindrical, and was downtown, to the west of the Hancock Building, to the east of the Willis Tower. This lovely, shimmering thing, with a single antenna atop it.

"Wow," she said.

"What?" Jon asked.

"That building," Meghan said. "When did that go up?"

Jon peered out the window, leaning his head down to do so. He was a tall man.

Leaning in, she could smell his cologne, musky and spicy. Jon always smelled good.

"Which one?" he asked.

"That one," she said. "The beautiful one."

She pointed, and a couple of the other commuters glanced out the window, to see what she was pointing at.

"I didn't even see them building it," she said.

Jon craned his neck, squinting. "I don't see it."

Meghan laughed. "Right. There."

It was catching the sunset light, this building. The window panes were delicate-seeming, but strong. Like dragon scales. She could see the turn of the building by the way they caught the waning light. And the single antenna atop it made the whole thing seem like a rocket to her.

Jon laughed. "The Sears Tower?"

"It's Willis, now," one of the other commuters said.

"Yeah, I know," Jon said. "I don't see it, Meghan."

"You need glasses, Jon," Meghan said. "It's silver and green. You absolutely can't miss it."

The train started up again, and made a turn, and downtown was lost to them.

Meghan shook her head.

"Dude, you totally missed it," she said. "It was beautiful."

"They're always building stuff downtown," Jon said. "I only notice when they tear a building down, anymore."

Meghan laughed, her shoulders shaking as she did.

It was gorgeous, that building.

When she got off at her stop (several stops ahead of Jon), she paused at the platform, looked again at that new building. The sky around it was dark, evening was descending, but still it caught the last rays of sunlight and shimmered.

She dug out her cell phone and snapped a shot of it, then looked at the picture. She couldn't wait to show Jon tomorrow.

Looking down at the little screen on her phone, she let out a gasp. There was nothing there: it wasn't there.

She looked back up, and could see the building. She snapped another photograph of it, and again, the building wasn't there.

"What the hell?" she asked aloud, alone on the platform at the moment.

Everything else was there, just not that building.

A third time, she looked up, and saw it once again.

When she got home, she turned on the evening news, the local reports, just to see if the building turned up in the broadcasts. But it didn't. There was the same old Loop skyline. Not a trace of the place. Then again, they didn't always do panoramic views of the city on the evening news.

So she went to the deck atop her building, which had been an old Freemason lodge one time, long ago, before somebody had done a gut rehab job on the place, turned it into a bunch of lofts. There was a rooftop deck for the tenants to enjoy, a nicely-sized couple of interlocking wooden squares that gave tenants a great view of downtown, albeit from a distance, from Lincoln Square, so it was distant.

But even from this shimmery distance, with night having fallen, she could see the building, shining and beautiful.

It was mesmerizing, that place, even though she couldn't understand how her camera couldn't capture it. Maybe it was made of some new material that was somehow resistant to photography?

On a whim, she dug out her cell phone and called up Nancy Lanegan, one of her friends, who lived farther south, right in Streeterville, with her rich boyfriend, Patrick Drosser, who worked at the Board of Trade.

They lived right downtown, and there was no way she couldn't see that building.

Her phone rang, and Nancy picked up.

"Hey, Meghan," Nancy said. "What's up?"

"Oh, hi," Meghan said, feeling like an idiot. "Have you seen that new building downtown?"

"The Trump Tower?" Nancy asked. "Ghastly. Like a giant corporate cock, swinging in the wind, no?"

Meghan laughed.

"No, not that one," she said. "It's west of Hancock, but east of Sears. It's greenish-silver."

Her friend was quiet a moment, like maybe she was looking out their window.

Their place faced south, faced the river.

"Is it north or south?"

"I don't know," Meghan said. "I can see it from my deck. I can't tell whether it's north or south of the river."

"Uhhh," Nancy said. "I don't see it. But we can only really see a sliver of downtown."

Meghan really wanted to ask her friend to go to her deck, to look properly, but she knew Nancy wouldn't do that for her.

"Okay," Meghan said. "I was just wondering."

She hung up and went downstairs, back to her place.

Then she went about making herself a Supreme Pizza for One, which was like peppers and sausage and pepperoni and onions and olives crammed in a smallish square. She had it with a glass of red wine, leafed through her mail.

Meghan turned on the television again, just to have some noise. She hated the sound of her own chewing. She ate most of the pizza, cut it like it was a Union Jack, a cross and a diagonal, so she got eight tiny pieces out of the original square, of which she ate half, saving the rest of it for tomorrow.

The newspeople talked about a meteor shower tonight, how it would be visible in the night's sky. Meghan liked that, thought it might give her another excuse to go up on the deck and look at the mystery building.

Instead, she put on some jeans and a green blouse, grabbed her coat, keys, and phone, and went out front to catch a bus downtown. It was crazy, she knew, but it bothered her, she had to know, had to see the building up close.

So, she sat on the bus with the other overlit apparitions, and went downtown. She was halfway kicking herself at having taken a bus, and not the El, and for even going back downtown on a workday, but she had to know, had to see it.

Past the blur of bars and restaurants she went ever-southward, until she got off the bus, just north of the river, because she really wasn't sure where that building was.

She hopped out and zipped up her jacket, as it was a little cool and breezy, and glanced at her watch: 7:11.

Meghan shook her head at her own silliness, dicking around downtown when she could have been home under a blanket, watching cable. Instead, she was playing Nancy Drew.

In the glass-and-steel canyons of downtown, she didn't know where the mystery building was. It was hard to get her bearings. Then she saw the Sears Tower, and just mentally projected where the other building should be, turning like she was a weathervane, pivoting.

This part of downtown was mostly quiet after hours, except for the restaurants, where affluent patrons stuffed their faces—young men in suits and their too-pretty-by-half dates in five-inch heels.

Meghan guessed that if she headed south across the river, she'd find the building, although she wasn't positive. Streetside, downtown, she was an ant walking between the legs of titans. The other buildings dwarfed her. She avoided downtown in winter, when great, deathly chunks of ice would fall from the great buildings, smashing on the sidewalk marked with yellow and black warning signs.

Meghan had a morbid fear of dying that way, although in early summer, as it was now, she had no worries, except perhaps for window-mounted air conditioners in some of the old brownstones. She feared those tumbling down upon her, and would walk guardedly, wondering how many people died that way. Or falling scaffolding. Maybe a meteorite would hit her. She shivered, wanted her brain to shut up about falling objects for awhile.

She crossed the river, the green, aquatic apparition that snaked through the city. The river so foul it was made to flow in reverse, so it wouldn't poison the lake with its toxins and its filth.

Cars whisked past as she went over the bridge, and Meghan thought she could feel the thing sway a tiny bit. She assumed bridges must have a little give to them, something in the nature of steel to bend without breaking.

On the other side, on Wacker Drive, she looked around again, took her bearings. Where was this place? Was it all a mirage? Or worse, a hallucination?

Then she saw it, just the tip of it, shining and bright. She walked down the street toward it, although when she made her way in the direction, the building vanished behind some of the other buildings, at least until she got to the clearing where the El trains went, and she could see it again.

Up closer as she was, the brightness, the silver-green color of it, was all the more apparent. The reticulated window tiles radiant and bright. The structure wasn't a perfect cylinder, not like she'd seen from the train. Rather, it was a stepped thing, with a broad cylindrical base, then a narrower column, and then a third column, narrower still, with the lone spire at the top. The building was massive.

How could she have missed it? Luminescent, opalescent. The thing was majestic, elegantly monstrous. She couldn't see inside the thing, despite all the light it was throwing off. The windows radiated light without being translucent.

It was amazing. She hadn't heard anything about it in the news, and as she walked up to it, she held up her cell phone camera to snap pictures of it. This time, up close. No way she could miss it. But the camera didn't see it.

It was unnerving; she held the camera up in front of her, and in the little thumbnail screen that mirrored what the camera's little eye saw, there was nothing there.

It was unmistakable. The phone really was blind to this thing. It wasn't possible, made Meghan's hands sweat, this contradiction. Looking through her phone, she saw only emptiness where the building stood.

A young couple walked by, a balding man and his black-haired girlfriend.

Meghan stopped them with a wave of her hand.

"Can you see that building?" she asked, pointing at the thing.

The young man glanced over his shoulder. "Which building?"

"That one, right there," she said. "Silver and green. Bright. Shiny. Tall."

"Sorry, Ma'am," he said, laughing. "I don't know what you're talking about."

"Yeah," the young woman said, her face very tan, a wrinkle or two of confusion at her forehead. "There's nothing there."

"Seriously? You can't see it?" she asked. They shook their heads, and walked away, whisper-chuckling to themselves.

Now Meghan was particularly worried. Was she losing her mind? Was that it? Seeing things?

She closed her phone and put it in her pocket, kept walking toward the building. Indeed, nobody seemed to be reacting to it, and the thing demanded attention, drew your eye. If they could see it, they would be reacting to it. It was beautiful, although the implication that she was the only one able to see it made her think perhaps it was horrible, too—a token of her losing her mind.

Now just perhaps a block or two away from the place, the thing loomed ever larger above her, seeming to be like a cathedral, majestic and awe-inspiring. And those odd, light-emitting tiles that were themselves opaque.

And people milling around downtown like it wasn't even there.

"Can't you see it?" said a man, hollering, waving at the thing. He was yelling at the people walking by, who were giving him a wide berth. He looked to be in his thirties, was wearing a suit, although his shirt was untucked, his tie was askew, and his yellow hair was tousled. "Anybody?"

He could see it.

Meghan felt a rush of hope in this realization, that she wasn't alone. She crossed the street, almost unmindful of any traffic, in her eagerness to catch up with the man, who held an attaché case in one hand, which he was brandishing at the building.

"It's right here, plain as fucking day!" the man said.

"I see it," Meghan called out, and the man paused.

This close, they were both colored green and silver by the thing, like standing too close to a fluorescent sign. Even the unseeing were colored by the light of the place, though they did not know this. Everybody's faces had that cadaverous glow about them, owing to the building.

"You do?" the man asked. Meghan nodded.

"Oh, thank God," he said. "None of these idiots see it."

"I know," Meghan said. This close the building was impossibly large, and she felt her usual urban angst hit her a bit at the foot of the place, although she was certain nothing would fall from this building.

"They can't see the noses on their faces," the man yelled, trying hard to stare down the people walking by. Meghan felt more than a little embarrassed by his yelling.

"What is it?" she asked.

"Can't see a damned thing!" he said. "Walking wounded! Walking dead! Blindman's Bluff, right? Human piñatas, just waiting for the stick to whack'em!"

He swung his attaché around him, wheeled about, his leather-soled oxfords scraping on the sidewalk as he moved.

Meghan stepped away from the man, looking instead at the building again, trying to see some name, something to identify it. There were great doors in the front of it. Revolving doors. But again, she couldn't properly see inside it. There was something sinuous above the door, a sculpture that called to mind an octopus.

"Full of candy," the man said. "Candy-coated souls! You can't see it! The sugar glaze across your eyes is blinding you! Hard as rock candy! Candy apple consciousness."

The tentacles of the thing wound down around the door, formed an archway. Meghan looked up at the building, dazzled by its light, by the perspective of it. It was like being at the feet of a god.

On a whim, she reached her hand out to touch the building, while the man jabbered behind her, while people walking by went out of their way to avoid them both.

Biting her lip, Meghan reached out, stretched her fingers, feeling for the building. She imagined it being cool to the touch. Monolithic. Like how she imagined a pyramid feeling. Antiquity.

Up close, this close, she could see the hint of sigils on the stone, in a language she could not comprehend.

The man stopped his yammering for a moment to watch her. His silence actually made her turn her head.

The script was completely unlike anything she'd ever seen. And as her eyes traveled up the stone, she saw that every single stone was covered by the angular alien script. In a building of this size, the amount of writing that would be covering it would be enormous. Who had done such a thing?

Her hand touched the building, her hand tingling against the stone, which felt surprisingly warm and butter-smooth. She'd never felt anything like it—smooth, except for where the sigils were, and even they felt smoother than anything she'd ever touched. Meghan traced the pattern of the thing with her fingertips, while the man looked on.

"It's real," Meghan said, with evident relief. "I can touch it."

"You've done it," the man said. "You actually have done it. Priestess-Prophet. Orderly ordainment. You see, Pharisees? She's *touching* what you can't even see."

People just detoured, walked around them, while the man looked on, watched Meghan stroke the stone, finding meaning in the material.

From down here, streetside, looking up, the building went on forever. The angles were so sharp, so steep, the abominable domination of wrongful geometry, claiming her.

"Did you touch it?" Meghan asked the man.

He shook his head like a dog after a bath.

"I don't have the guts," he said. "But I see it. I see you."

A final time, Meghan took out her phone, held it up, went to take a picture, and saw that the phone could not see this building that was right in front of her.

"Not possible," Meghan said. "It's insane. Or I am."

She put the phone away, let go of the building, and walked up to the door, gazed at the octopoid thing that draped itself around the entrance. It was not a welcoming thing.

"I'm going in," Meghan said. The revolving door looked to be made of brass, each space between it colored by smoked glass.

"She's going in," the man said. "You see?"

Meghan wondered what would happen—if she entered the building that nobody else could see, would she, too, disappear from view? Would they see her vanish? What would become of her?

"Come with me," Meghan said to the man, who again shook his head violently, vehemently.

"I'm afraid I can't," he said. "Haven't got the stones, I lack the sand, haven't the grit for it. I'm here to harangue the human gobstoppers. You're the Prophet; I'm only the Deacon."

"I'm not afraid," Meghan said. "It's just a place."

"A place nobody can see," the Deacon said. "Only you and me."

Meghan was not comforted by this, that the only other person who could apparently see the building was a raving madman.

She stood by the door, turned to look at the pedestrians moving past them, the madman watching her, them, everything. Fat couples, young people, city folk, suburbanites, walking, looking, gawking, staring at her, at them.

"Hey," Meghan said, calling out to get their attention. She wanted them to see. It took three tries to drag their eyes to her location. "Watch this."

And she shoved past the revolving door of brass and smoked glass, and went into the place, hoping that the blind bastards saw something they could not explain, something that would haunt them for the rest of their days, something inexplicable, something bizarre and mysterious, enigmatic and incomprehensible, miraculous and horrifying.

A true disappearing act.

Sometimes Meghan felt like she didn't even exist.

And today, just this once, she was right.

The Rocket's Red Glare

1

PRESIDENT BIFF DIXON had words for everybody. Victor Tremble thought this while watching the man bring his burnished tan and baritone voice to bear on everybody on the trideo. He was the talking head's talking head, the white hair at his temples only making him seem more statesmanlike.

"Faithful patriots," President Dixon said, that Southern-fried drawl like a familiar aroma in a well-used country kitchen. "As you know, we have been populating the Martian Colonies. Already, around 25 million brave adventurers have been processed through Space Station Liberty to be resettled in the American Martian Colony (AMC). This ensures an American foothold on Mars has brought that the blessings of liberty and freedom extend into the heavens themselves. The Red Planet is now Red, White, and Blue—thanks to you."

Victor wanted to switch off the President, but the Smart-visions didn't let you preempt Presidential addresses, so he got his cane and limped his way to his kitchenette while the man spoke.

He wondered if Dixon was even still alive. He remembered him being elected about 20 years ago, back when Victor went off to fight Gulf War VI in the Republic of Frackistan, trying to wring the last drops of oil from the region.

Dixon had promised a swift and easy victory in Frackistan. It had gotten him elected, and he'd gotten so cozy in the White House, he just stayed on, heading the New American Christianist Party (NACP). How many terms was it? Victor did the math in his head. Five terms. And Dixon looked about the same as he ever did. Maybe they just wanted him to look the same, to keep everybody reassured. Maybe they hired a lookalike to represent him. Maybe he was an on-screen simulation, powered by artificial intelligence. Maybe he was a hologram. Maybe he'd always been one.

Victor mixed himself a Détente, even treated himself to some ice, while Dixon spoke.

"Space is real dangerous, my friends. We know this. You know this. The bravery and sacrifice of these New American colonists has ensured a more prosperous nation at home. You go up there, so we can live better down here," Dixon said, pointing upward and downward with a tanned and manicured index finger. "And the AMC administrator Donald Hough told me that there is room in the colony for about five million more Americans. That's it. It's all that's left up there in the heavens."

That gave Victor pause, roughly mid-pour. The American Colonial Administrative Agency (ACAA) had sent him an informational flier about it, both digitally and hard copy. It told him that he'd been selected for it, and what an honor it would be for him to take part in the New American colonization of Mars.

He had applied for the AMC, since it was some place to go, something to do. It wasn't quite that glib a decision, but he had nothing left for him on Earth, figured he might as well give Mars a try. His best buddy from the war, Carl Farber, had been on the first rocket up, years ago. He'd talked to Carl a few times. With the distance between Earth and Mars, a bit over 72 million miles, communication had a lag that could go as much as 20 minutes. Sometimes only five minutes if the planets were well aligned. It made communication tricky. But he'd talked to Carl.

He looked good, despite the fragmented display. He looked like himself.

"Carl," Victor said. "You son of a bitch. Nice of you to take my call. I can't believe they took you."

Carl had won the Silver Star for bravery in Frackistan, had lost both his legs. They'd been replaced by high-tensile polyuminum prostheses. Once he'd learned how to walk on them, Carl swore that they were better than his old legs. Victor mixed himself a drink while waiting for Carl's reply.

"Believe it, Vic," Carl said. "It's great here. You should come. It's unbelievable what they have here. You should do it. Look, I gotta go. Demand for the phone is high, and one thing I learned early on is you have to be good to your fellow colonists. Anyway, great seeing you, Vic. Miss you, buddy."

The call ended, and Victor was happy to have seen his friend. He'd called him twice more over the years. The reports were always good. Life was hard up there, but life was good. It felt good to break new ground, to be blazing a trail. To leave all the craziness on Earth behind.

"I'm a Martian, now," Carl said. "We all are. Martians. It changes you. You should fill out the questionnaire. I bet they'd take you."

"What's it like out there?" Victor asked, waiting for Carl's response. The waiting was what made conversations with Mars challenging, even for somebody with patience. Victor never considered himself one of those patient people. Not here, not in Frackistan. It wasn't in his makeup. He kept occupied while waiting for Carl's reply. He wondered how much all of that cost the Martian Colony, paying for the precious communication back and forth.

"Cold," Carl said. "Not gonna lie. I mean, we have climate control, but you never quite get past it. And dusty. We have to detox any time we're out of the domes. All the perchlorate. You never stop hearing about that. But we're making progress. Everybody is. You should be up here, Bro."

"I'll consider it," Victor said. "It's not like I've got much here, not anymore."

He hit SEND before he could think of anything else to say. Carl's communiques were always so neatly encapsulated. But that's how Carl was. He'd been a tidy guy, even in Frackistan. No loose ends. Even though that place had been one giant loose end, Carl had been the only one to keep it together, at least until he was blown apart.

Still, they'd put him back together, the way they all had. Victor had no complaints. The Polygon provided good pensions for wounded veterans. He could get the care he needed, when he needed. And Frackistan just kept on going.

Carl's response came quicker, around five minutes after Victor's.

"Never mind all that, Bro," Carl said. "Come to Mars. We'll get everything sorted out, I promise you. Nothing's as bad as Frackistan."

2

Nothing's as bad as Frackistan. That was something all the vets told themselves and each other, the ones who'd been unfortunate enough to fight in that endless war. Some historians called it the 50 Years' War, although it had moved past that point—it was like the historians had gotten tired of keeping track of it.

The partisans of Frackistan lived in caves, hid from the drones, came out at odd moments, decisive moments, and killed the New American Army regulars when they could. No amount of night vision and high tech surveillance could stop them, it seemed.

The AMC questionnaire had been astonishingly thorough, with ridiculously invasive questions that had bothered Victor, more because he couldn't really remember the answers to them.

His favorite childhood vacation?

Any pets? If so, their names and when they died.

Favorite foods, colors, jobs.

Least-favorite things.

On and on. Like 250 questions. He'd filled them all out, too, sent the thing away, kept waiting for his number to come up, and yet, still, nothing.

He mixed his drink and sat and watched the President talk. That tan skin, those incredibly white teeth. He wondered if they doctored his image for broadcast. Nobody looked that good for that long, especially nobody that tan. And "good" was only applicable in the loosest possible context. He just didn't look decrepit. That passed for good, in Victor's eyes.

"The Colonial Emigration Administration is going to be sending agents to interview prospective candidates, so that we can round out our Mars mission with the finest this country has to offer. Space is dangerous. We all know this. But we'll do it, because whatever we set our minds to, we do it. God Bless 'Murica."

With that, the broadcast went back to the normal trideo programming, with *What's For Lunch?* popping on, to the usual drone of automated laughter. Victor flicked off the trideo, limped over to the window, gazed out across New Funswick, watched the people below walk by. Nobody ever looked up, not in the city.

There were so many beautiful people.

Everybody was young and lovely.

Unlined faces—unlined from youth, from lack of worry, from lack of intelligence.

New Funswick was a sea of blankly beautiful faces.

The men were all churning like pistons, the women prancing along pneumatically, everything honed, strong, and taut. The future of America was cut—not die-cut, but chiseled by surgical hands, personal trainers, and punitive fitness regimens. They were an army of athleticism, part of Dixon's Fittest Americans Report, and the War on Obesity, which, along with Gulf War VI, was America's longest, hardest war. But unlike Frackistan, the War on Obesity was apparently being won, from the look of everybody.

Victor sipped his drink and looked on with emotions even he couldn't fully place. Envy? Contempt? There was something contemptible in youth, the openness of faces, the absence of scars.

This was a generation untried, untested, unworried, unfettered.

For all of their gym-sculpted physiques, these were not soldiers, were not mothers and fathers. They were children, still, walking around in adult bodies, playing grownup games.

Fucking everybody was young. They all were. There wasn't an old lady around, not a vagrant, nothing. Just clean-living, fit mannequins, enjoying life. The AMC had recruited older astronauts, and had a nondiscrimination policy for the disabled. Space was dangerous. They said it on their promotional materials. The marketing drew risk takers. The people he saw trotting around New Funswick weren't risk takers. They were lambs.

"What do you do all day?" Victor asked them through the window, setting his drink on the ledge. "Who *are* you people?"

The America he had defended in Gulf War VI was not the America he saw down there, nourished on Biff Dixon's well-oiled lines and spoon-fed cornpone dominion theology by way of the NACP's relentless infographic messaging. It had been a different place, and it had changed when he had come home.

Or else he had changed.

Maybe it was a bit of both. Frackistan had that way with people.

There was a knock at his door, three pert raps. It would only mean one thing: his sister, Antigone, had turned up for her weekly wellness check-in of him.

Part of him thought about pretending he wasn't home, but she'd know he was home. He was always home. He could hear her fishing out her key card, opening the door.

In she came, as perky as ever. Ten years younger than he was, with pink hair styled in a short, pixielike cut, her big brown eyes combing his place even as her wide mouth broke into an ingratiating smile, she shut the door and doffed her striped tiger overcoat and walked over, giving him a hug.

"Vic," Antigone said, embracing him warmly. "I knew you wouldn't answer, so I just let myself in."

Antigone always did that, narrated what was obvious and apparent. She was wearing jeggings and a black sweater, had a silver fitwatch at her wrist, taking her pulse, monitoring her.

She took a seat in his living room, crossed a leg, looked him over.

"I brought you some treats," Antigone said. "From Stellario's. Elephant ears."

"Thanks, Anti," Victor said. He'd called her that since they'd been kids.

She looked around his place, the way she always did. Taking it all in. She worked as User Experience consultant at Synergesia, a tech company.

"You didn't have to drop by," he said.

"Of course I did, Vic," Antigone said. "I wouldn't let anything happen to you."

She was that way the whole time he'd come back from Frackistan. When she'd seen his wounded leg. That's how he saw it, even though his leg was gone. It was wounded. The wound had made it disappear, replaced by the prosthetic.

"We're in New Funswick," Victor said. "Nothing can happen to me here."

"Things can happen anywhere," Antigone said. "Mom and dad made me promise to look out for you."

Their folks had died years ago, and it was absurd to Victor that his baby sister would have to look out for him. They'd always danced around him when he'd come back from Frackistan. None of them understood that what he'd seen there, what he'd done there, was worse than anything in New Funswick. New Funswick was a party by comparison. He'd seen whole villages annihilated by Purefire missiles. The whoosh of hot air from them, the clouds of dust, the shockwave and the blue-white fireball that set everything alight. There weren't even any screams, because the air was all gobbled up by the missile. There was just that horrible fire, and the burning bodies, the ones who'd not been blown apart by the first blast.

"I don't need looking after," Victor said. "Anti, you need your own life."

"I have my own life," Antigone said, giving him a swat. "You're part of it, whether you want to be or not."

Now was as good a time as any to mention it.

"I'm thinking of going to Mars," Victor said. Antigone looked at him like he was crazy.

"What?"

"You heard me," Victor said. "You know, a new start."

"You'd leave me behind here on Earth?" Antigone asked, a plaintive pitch to her voice. She was the sort of person who needed to be needed.

"It's not a matter of leaving you behind, per se," Victor said. "Some of my buddies are out there. The lower gravity helps. You know, with these."

He tapped his prosthetic.

"Lower gravity," Antigone said, scoffing. "It's dusty out there. And cold. And it's a colony. It's not like here. You'd hate it up there."

"I hate it here," Victor said, watching her get up, pacing. She was so young, still. She needed to settle down, start a family. Build something, rather than tending to her war-ravaged big brother. He wasn't going to say it, but he sure as hell was thinking it.

"Oh, stop," Antigone said. "This is your home. Not out there."

"Frackistan changed all of that," Victor said. "I don't even feel at home in my own skin, anymore. At least Mars, well, it's got nothing to do with Gulf War VI. It's new territory. Something for me to wrap my head around. All I have here are memories."

"And me," Antigone said. "You've got me."

"Of course," Victor said. "And I'll always have you. And be grateful to you. Besides, we can keep in touch from Mars. I've talked to my buddy Carl a bunch of times. The AMC is good about keeping in touch with friends and family."

Antigone stopped pacing and walked over, touching Victor's weatherworn face with her soft, pale hand. Her fingernails were painted pink, a perfect match for her hair.

"If this is what you want, you know I can't stop you," Antigone said. "But it just sounds bad and sad to me. You should stay here, not fly off into space. I mean, I've seen the stories. They work out there. It's hard work. We're talking about, what, terraforming a planet? It's harsh."

"I've dealt with harsh before," Victor said. "I'm comfortable with harsh. All of this around here? It's soft. It makes me soft. I can't afford to be soft."

The disability pension he earned wasn't ample, but it was steady. That, and his meritorious service stipend for serving with courage and honor in war, it gave him a comfortable living in New Funswick. Better than he'd have had before the war, that was for sure.

"You've done your service," Antigone said. "You deserve to take it easy, Vic."

"I'm a fighter, Anti," Victor said. "I have to fight. The fight is part of it for me. You take away the fight, and part of me dies with it."

Antigone resumed her pacing, grimacing. "Let's not talk about dying, Vic. I mean, if you want to go to Mars, go to Mars. But I'm saying you still have a life here. You have a sister who loves you. Right here."

"And I'd have that on Mars, too," Victor said. "The country's changing. I feel like a ghost. Everybody's getting younger, I'm getting older. And people see me, they think of the war. They don't like it. I stand out in ways I don't like. At least on Mars, I can lend some service, maybe make amends for things I did in Frackistan. Bad things."

Nobody called them "war crimes" anymore. Not that he committed any. But Biff Dixon had eliminated the notion of war crimes from the New American vocabulary. They didn't exist.

"All's fair in war," Dixon would said, if anybody dared question it. "I'm not about to tie New Americans soldiers' hands behind their backs in time of war. This is a war for the survival of our way of life. Our boys need to be able to fight freely for freedom. You think those bomb jockeys in Frackistan care about war crimes? They don't."

"That's all in the past, Vic," Antigone said. "You could find a woman. Fall in love. Something like that."

He knew Antigone wanted to help. She always wanted to help. She was a healer. She sought harmony and order. Chaos made her uncomfortable. Dischord disturbed her.

"All I see here is Frackistan," Victor said. "Oil fires. Mass killings. Bombs. Drones. Explosions. Death. That's all I have here. Even here, in New Funswick. That's what I see. Mars is a blank slate. It's dusty, but it's clean. Earth is a graveyard. There's no wars up on Mars."

"Not yet," Antigone said. "Once they make it nice, there will be."

"Maybe," Victor said. He laughed a little to himself, a wheezy rasp. "Yeah, you're probably right about that. Right now, nobody can afford a war up there. It's too expensive. But, as I see it, there's a chance at building something up there. Something new, something better. Maybe we'll make a mess of it like we did Earth, but there's at least hope up there. I feel it, that bit of hope."

Antigone teared up, walked over and hugged him.

"I hope you don't go," she said. "I hope you stay here, where you belong."

3

His door buzzed, somebody out there, pushing the button. Victor glanced at his wallclock, which told him that it was 1820 hours. The evening sun was shining through his place, orange-hued, wearing smog like an evening gown.

"Coming," Victor said, limping over. He toggled the peep-cam, saw there was a fit young man in a business suit standing there on the little screen. He flipped the intercom switch. "Yeah?"

"Mr. Tremble?" the man asked. "I'm Quinn Hendricks, of the Colonial Emigration Administration. Can I talk with you a minute?"

A CEA man here? Victor looked around his little place. He hadn't planned on company. Then again, he never planned on it. And, aside from Antigone, he never had any.

"Sure, just a second," he said. He limped over to one of his free chairs, tossed away a bag that had been sitting there. Then he went back to the door and he opened it.

Mr. Hendricks was standing there in his blue-grey suit, the red CEA badge at his lapel. He was carrying an aluminum attaché that had the CEA logo embossed on it—a red ball, dotted with blue and white stars.

"What is this about?" Victor asked.

"Your application, sir," Hendricks said. "May I come in and talk with you about it a bit?"

"Sure," Victor said, gesturing. He moved aside so the guy could enter the room. Quinn took the seat that Victor had hoped he would, and he limped over to his favorite chair, an old rocker that had been his great-great-grandmother's.

Hendricks was tan, himself, with short-cut blond hair. He looked maybe 28 years old. He opened the case and took out a thick red file folder, set it in his lap, looking expectantly at Victor.

"Is there a problem?" Victor asked.

"No problem, sir," Hendricks said. The orange sunlight had turned to a dusky red that filled the room. Hendricks seemed to notice it, nodding, chuckling. "Better get used to that color, Mr. Tremble. You're going to Mars."

"I am?"

Hendricks could see that disbelief on Victor's face. "It's true. We're sorry it took this long to get to you processed, in all honesty. A decorated war veteran, three tours in Frackistan, wounded honorably in combat. Exemplary. Just what we need up on Mars."

"Yeah?"

Hendricks nodded. "We need all sorts up there, of course. The lower gravity will make it easier on your leg, although you have to be careful about that. There's a whole primer on life on Mars, which you'll receive as part of your Colonial Resettlement Package, which should be arriving in the mail in the next few days."

"You came here personally to tell me that I'm in?" Victor asked. "Since when was I so important?"

"Oh, we visit each colonist personally, Mr. Tremble," Hendricks said. "We always have to be sure that the resident applicant is the lawful person who applied. Would you believe we've actually had people try to defraud their way to the Colonies? Everybody wants to go up there, but the ACAA has very strict parameters on who gets to go."

Victor hardly heard the kid.

He was going to Mars. He was already trying to figure out how he'd break the news to Antigone.

"Okay, wait," Victor said. "I'm crippled—"

"Wounded In Combat," Hendricks said. "Yes, we know that. We have plenty of WICs at the AMC. They love it up there. Your war buddy, Carl Farber, was one of the first to go."

Victor had remembered when Carl volunteered for the mission, envying his friend's opportunity. He'd have to call Carl again, tell him about it. Calls to Mars were expensive, and even with his disability pension, Victor really couldn't spare it, but for this, it was worth it.

"What sort of job would I have up there?" Victor asked.

"The AMC has mostly terraforming jobs these days," Hendricks said. "I'm not talking digging with shovels, here. Rather, it's rig-driving: exosuits, that kind of thing. Work that doesn't require a healthy body so much as a steady hand.

And you, sir, strike me as a very steady man. Are you a steady man?"

"Uh," Victor said. He remembered taking the shrapnel from the Trussian Frackistani smartmine, the damned thing hopping after their squad like an overeager dog in a game of deadly fetch. He hadn't felt so steady then.

Hendricks held up a light pen, shined the light in Victor's eyes, moved it this way and that. Victor followed it, squinting.

"What's that for?"

"Just a routine test, sir," Hendricks said. "Have to be sure."

"Sure of what?"

Hendricks's open face snapped shut a moment. "I'm afraid that's classified, sir."

"Okay," Victor said.

Hendricks put away the light pen, then fished out a flatscreen pad and a stylus, handed it to Victor, after touching a button that made the blank screen flit to life, showing various documents on display within it, trapped under touch-sensitive photoglass.

"I'm just going to need you to sign these, in triplicate, unfortunately. Everything's in triplicate these days, sir," Hendricks said. "Accountability, you know."

"What are these?"

"A Confirmation of Identity (COI) form, a liability waiver, a resettlement fund contract, that kind of thing," Hendricks said. "It's all very routine."

"Should I get a lawyer to look at these?" Victor asked.

Hendricks didn't blink. "If you like. We've been through millions of these but do what you feel is best. Do you have a lawyer?"

"No," Victor admitted. "I'm not made of money."

"Few people are these days," Hendricks said. "Only the best people are, anyway."

"Right," Victor said. He wanted to vomit when he thought about the handful of trillionaires running the nation. What did trillionaires even do? Probably turn their noses up at the billionaires and millionaires. What came after trillionaires? Quadrillionaires. They'd be even worse.

Victor thought about it, stylus in hand.

Hendricks waited in silence.

"Of course, there are only so many seats left on this last batch of rockets," Hendricks said. "You want to get in on the front end on this, versus getting tangled up in paperwork and left behind, believe me."

"The front end of the back end?" Victor asked, smirking at the kid.

"The rearguard, if you prefer," Hendricks said, unblinking. Him using a term like that, when he'd never been anywhere near a battlefield.

"Rearguard," Victor grumbled.

The kid just sat there, face half in shadow, and half lit by the waning sun.

"There won't be any more after this?" Victor asked.

"Not for awhile," Hendricks said. "The AMC can only support so many people. Mars is so much smaller of a planet, and with China, India, Brazil, Japan, and the EU up there, our slice of it isn't conducive to larger-scale operations. Carrying capacity is everything."

"Carrying capacity?"

"What Mars can sustain," Hendricks said. "What our own country can handle. These operations are horribly expensive. It's far cheaper to send unmanned ships out there, don't you know? Astronauts are expensive. Colonists are expensive."

"Everything's expensive," Victor said. "Fuck it."

He signed the documents, used a digital thumbprint to confirm that he was, in fact, the signatory. Hendricks seemed quietly satisfied by this, the concern etching his young face giving way to something else.

"I think it's very brave, what you're doing, here," Hendricks said. "You're guaranteeing a future for this great country of ours, you know."

Tremble looked the young man in the eye, saw mostly flatness, no warmth he could measure or comprehend. He just shook Victor's hand, a cold and papery grip.

"Your materials will be arriving in a day or so, sir," Hendricks said.

"What happens to my place, here?" Victor asked.

"It's covered in the relocation document," Hendricks said, producing a diskette for Victor, emblazoned with the AMC logo. "It's all here."

Victor took the tiny diskette. His whole life was on a wafer of opalescent plastic.

"God Bless America," Hendricks said.

"God Bless America," Victor said, showing him the door.

4

The rockets to Mars traveled almost daily. Victor could see the broadcasts of their launching, the excited, happy would-be colonists knifing through the sky in powerful Ares rockets, vaulted skyward using a massive railgun at Cape Carnival.

The clips showed happy, vigorous colonists in blue ACAA jumpsuits, walking in slow motion toward the gleaming rockets, while patriotic music played. Not the everyday stuff they used, but bold, brazen, world-conquering sorts of anthems, the kind of music they trotted out during military parades. The kind of music that drove Victor to enlist in the first place, filling his head and his heart with courage.

In his excitement, Victor had read up about the specifications of the Ares rocket. It turned out to be pretty light on fuel, relying on the force of the railgun platform to get it into space, as a form of projectile. From there, on it sped toward Mars, carrying its payload of colonists, to be delivered according to the rigorous, relentless timetables mandated by the American Colonial Administrative Agency.

Victor was surprised at the choice of the Ares rocket as the delivery vehicle, as it had been originally intended as an intercontinental ballistic missile, before the ACAA had requisitioned them for the Mars Colonial Initiative.

It had been part of President Dixon's reorganization efforts, his Fittest Americans Report (FAR). Some scientists and engineers had objected to the choice of rockets, but they'd been quickly silenced and/or marginalized by the NACP. Once it had been clear that a steep price was paid for questioning Dixon's FAR, the protests died down.

"The problem is that there's just too many people on Earth," Dixon said. "We gotta branch out, stretch our legs a little, give ourselves more elbow room. Mother Earth is bursting at the seams. We gotta give her a little breathing space. I can't speak for those other countries, but 'Murica is doing her part, by God."

Victor had received his bus pass for the ACAA Training Program. It would be a week of intensive training intended to make him fit for Colonial life. A week seemed hardly sufficient in Victor's mind, but he wasn't about to lose his place in line.

To have been selected at all, to be given a second chance, was something Victor had not dared hope for. To be among the final offloading of colonists to Mars? To get away from the wars, famine, slaughter and death of Earth? It was like a dream.

And dreaming was what Victor did, remembering his days in Frackistan, the lost years, the endless war that had left the region a pulverized wasteland. They'd stopped calling it a proper country decades ago. It had become Frackistan to all of the soldiers tasked with fighting it. On and on. Whatever it had been, it was Frackistan, now.

Victor had been a Combat Exosuit Operator, First Class. That was a heady gig. As a CEO, he carried serious ordnance: that Fairchild 20 mm autocannon perched on his shoulder, with his secondary .50 caliber arm guns. The ammo loadout itself was a couple of tons. But his old Warhound combat chassis could bear the load, and Victor could, too. He enjoyed the work at first, despite the ongoing hellishness of it. Everything about Frackistan was bad.

The Warhound could take a beating. As did Victor. He missed that old exosuit. In a way, he missed the war, too, despite everything. Frackistan had been like a warm, if bloodied, blanket that had covered him for a decade of his life. It was a clear enemy. Knowing that there was somebody he was permitted—even encouraged—to kill made all the difference. Back home, with all the pretty kids walking around in astringent NACP peace and harmony, it just wasn't the same.

Looking at his finances to be sure he could afford it, he dialed up Carl Farber. Victor remembered being envious of Carl at getting in early that way. But as a thrice-decorated double amputee, Farber had been a natural for that kind of gig. Danger meant nothing to a man like Carl Farber.

The ACAA processed his dial-in request. There was that characteristic delay in communication with Mars, so Victor made himself another Détente and sipped it while he waited, setting his phone on the table next to his chair.

The tridphone screen flickered a moment, and there was Carl, grinning at him.

"Hey, Tremble," Farber said. "To what do I owe this dubious honor?"

"Hey, you son of a bitch," Victor said. "I'm coming to Mars. I just signed the paperwork. I'm going to be there."

He hit SEND and went back to his drink, waiting. He was used to the slow grind of Earth-to-Martian communication. He imagined making calls with Antigone this way. It would drive her crazy, he was sure.

"That's great," Farber said, giving a thumb's up. "It's great up here, Tremble. I don't care what they say. It's no harder than it was back on Earth. Hell, with the lower gravity, it's easier to get around. And the women don't mind. They *like* combat veterans up here."

Farber looked the same as ever—the same cleft chin and tanned face, the same ice-blue eyes and sand-hued hair. Farber was always the ruggedly handsome one, the man who even Frackistan couldn't touch—beyond taking both his legs, which Victor and Carl used to joke was Frackistan's revenge on him for daring to survive.

"Mars agrees with you, you son of a bitch," Victor said. "You look the same as you did before blastoff. Anyway, these calls are expensive, but I just wanted to let you know that I'm heading up there, so you better watch out. I'm cutting in on your Martian monopoly. Have the Chinese and Indians taken all the good spots, or is there still good land for us?"

Victor waited again, gave his Détente a good swig, flipped on the trideo newsfeed while waiting for Farber's reply. The war in Frackistan was continuing, with a company of exosuit-wearing soldiers blasting a ruined village into pebbles in an effort to snuff out the extremists. The chatter of the autoguns brought back memories fond and foul. Farber's reply came back.

"I love Mars, Tremble. You will, too. And, no, the Chinese and the Indians haven't taken all the good spots. Americans are making this place American. It's going from a red planet to a red, white, and blue planet, just like Dixon says. You take care of yourself, Tremble. I'll see you soon, Brother."

The connection terminated, and the ACAA deducted the cost of the call from Victor's bank account. It was money he could hardly spare, but he couldn't imagine going to Mars without at least giving Farber a head's up.

He finished his Détente and watched a rerun of *It's Not My Fault* until he fell asleep.

5

Antigone wasn't thrilled that he'd joined the Program. He'd told her about it already, but she brought it up again when they were having brunch at Bilko's. They'd gotten in there early, while the milling crowds gathered.

"I think it's crazy," Antigone said. "I think you're crazy. Can't you just relax and retire gracefully, Vic?"

He ate some eggscramble and shook his head.

"Anti, that's the point," Victor said. "I'm not made for retirement. I'm, you know, made for other things. I'm still a soldier."

"You're a veteran," Antigone said. "That's what you are. You did your service. You're willfully putting your head back in the lion's mouth by going out there. It's dangerous in space."

"It's dangerous here," Victor said. "I could get run over by a bus while crossing the street. Life is danger."

Antigone remained unconvinced, kept spearing melon balls with her fork before replying, until she had three in a row.

"It's not the same, and you know it," Antigone said. "And what is it about that space program, anyway? I've seen the footage—they send old people, and differently abled people up there."

He'd already read about it in the manual, their explanations.

"It's because it's so dangerous that they're doing that," Victor said. "They don't want to send young people up there—hell, they'd turn Mars into some kind of astro-orgy if you got a bunch of young people up there. The last thing they need at this stage is some Martian baby boom. They're sending old and infirm up there, folks who've been around the block a time or two and want an opportunity to serve their country one more time. We're saving humanity."

Antigone ate the orange melon balls, one by one.

"You sound like the NACP spokespeople," Antigone said, half-whispering it. You never knew where an NACP agent might be.

6

The AMC training was perfunctory. It didn't come even close to the training he underwent for Frackistan. As a veteran, there wasn't anything that Victor hadn't already seen over in Frackistan, and there wasn't anything the dead-eyed technicians at the AMC could throw at him that he couldn't handle.

The other would-be colonists were more hard-pressed than Victor to weather the training, which was mostly about navigating low-gravity environments and proper workplace safety protocols for life within confined spaces. A portion of the training involved preparation for being launched by a railgun into outer space. There was an entertaining session on extraplanetary diseases, and how to avoid them.

With the training broken up into the physical and psychological portions of the colonial enterprise, Victor surveyed the other colonists.

There was an even mix of men and women, most of them around his age, a few of them younger. They all had been given blue jumpsuits that bore the ACAA logo. There didn't appear to be any identifiable combat veterans among them, although Victor did notice one thing, however:

Four of the colonists were blind. Three were deaf. Eleven were physically handicapped in some way—seven wheelchair-bound, four (including himself) had canes or walkers.

One of the women, a pretty young woman with brown hair and hazel eyes, watched Victor watching them.

"I'm Melanie," she said. "I'm very excited about this."

"Yeah," Victor said. "I just am surprised. I assumed I'd be the only handicapped on this flight."

Melanie looked around them, surveyed the room. "There are lots of jobs differently abled people can do on Mars, sir. It's very high tech."

"Right," Victor said. "I'm Victor, by the way."

"Nice to meet you, Victor," Melanie said, snapping a hand out for him to shake. Her eyes flicked to his veterans patch on his shirt. "So, you served in Frackistan?"

"Ten years," Victor said. "Probably before you were born."

"Yeah, so," Melanie said. "I think this would be easy for somebody who survived that."

"That's what I was thinking," Victor said. "I just can't figure what some blind people are going to be doing on Mars. Don't they have a cure for blindness, yet?"

"I'm sure the ACAA has it figured out. They know just what they need up there," Melanie said.

"So, what's your story?" Victor said. "Why in the hell would you leave Earth behind for Mars?"

"My therapist recommended it," Melanie said.

"Your therapist recommended you go to Mars?" Victor said. "That seems extreme."

"Not for me," Melanie said. "I'm, you know, suicidal."

Halfway ashamed, she pulled the sleeves up on her blue jumpsuit, showing scars crisscrossing her wrists. They looked like old roads paved by uncertain city planners.

"Whoa," Victor said.

"Cries for help, I know," Melanie said. "I've heard it all before. But my therapist said this would be good for me. A fresh start. Everyone deserves a fresh start. America is all about fresh starts, isn't it?"

"Right," Victor said, waving over one of the technicians, who was a young man with a particularly flat gaze. His nametag simply said SPENCER in white letters on black plastic.

"What can I help you with, First Sergeant Tremble?" Spencer asked.

"Why are there so many handicapped on this flight?" Victor asked. Spencer just looked at him.

"I'm not responsible for the crew composition, Sergeant," Spencer said. "I'm only here to train colonists."

Melanie shrugged, tapped her forehead with a long and delicate digit. "He's a veteran. Probably a little PTSD going on in there."

"I'm just saying," Victor said. "What does Mars need blind people for? It's dangerous enough up there on its own, right?"

Spencer looked at the blind candidates, who were talking with each other in a close-knit group.

"Space is dangerous, Sergeant. I don't draw up the manifests," Spencer said. "I'm only here to train candidates."

"Training," Victor scoffed. "Right."

"Something to do with the lower gravity, is my guess," Melanie said, trying to be what she considered helpful.

"I don't see how lower gravity is going to help with blindness," Victor said.

"Doesn't it mean they have other senses? You know, like extra-acute senses?" Melanie asked. Spencer the dead-eyed technician had already ghosted elsewhere.

"I don't think that's true," Victor said, watching the blind candidates listening intently to the instructions provided to them by another tech who looked about as sallow as Spencer had.

"I'm sure ACAA has it all figured out," Melanie said. "I'm so excited about this trip. I'm anxious, too. I get anxious."

"It'll be fine," Victor said. "Just different."

4.

Days away from his own launch, Victor watched another fleet of Mars rockets launch, clicking through on the trideo. The railgun would vault them into the sky and into orbit, moving at incredible velocity.

It was very different from the rocket launches he remembered as a child, with all the noise and fire. The railgun launches were nearly noiseless humming surges by comparison. Only a stack of sonic booms marked the passage of the rockets into space.

Once in space, the rockets would fire, further propelling them toward Mars at even greater acceleration rates. Thanks to the program, the trip to Mars could be undertaken in a matter of months.

He watched the clips, could see the rockets arriving and safely landing, could see the new colonists embarking on their Martian adventure. The ACAA had made the enterprise almost routine. Years after the first colonists had arrived, it was something most Americans didn't think about that much.

Out of sight, out of mind—that's how it went these days. Up, up, and away.

He decided to splurge, gave Carl another call on the tridphone.

"Carl, you son of a bitch, I'm leaving in three days," Victor said, sending, waiting for Carl's reply. Carl's face snapped into a smile seven minutes later, his frozen face shifting to his characteristic grin.

"Can't wait to see you, you bastard," Carl said. "We'll roll out the welcome mat. There's whores up here, Vic. Martian whores. Not real Martians. American, though. American Martians."

Seeing his friend beaming at him made Victor long to make the trip.

"Hey, they're sending a bunch of blind people on my flight," Victor said. "What are blind people doing up on Mars?"

He waited for the response.

"The same thing anybody does on Mars," Carl said. "They survive. Everything's high tech up here, you bastard. The sky's the limit. They'll find something for them to do, don't you worry. Everybody does their part."

Victor watched the tridphone fee stack up, but, since he planned for this to be his last call from Earth, he indulged himself. Seeing Carl made him nostalgic. Friends were hard to come by, and friends who'd endured Frackistan, even more so.

"I was thinking about Lucky Valdez the other day," Victor said. "What a son of a bitch he was, right?"

He poured himself a Détente, waited for his friend's reply.

"Yeah, that Lucky, what a son of a bitch he was," Carl said, smiling. "A real son of a bitch."

"Whatever happened to him?" Victor asked in reply. He knew the answer, of course. He waited for seven minutes, just to see what Carl would say.

The tridphone served up a CONNECTION LOST message, and, when he tried to redial Carl, he was unable to reach him. Victor finished his cocktail, set the glass down on the table, and brooded, his hands shaking.

There was no Lucky Valdez.

Lucky Valdez was a secret code he and Carl had shared in Frackistan. It meant you had fucked up through no fault of your own. If Lucky Valdez came a-calling, it meant you were in a world of hurt.

Carl would have known that. He should have known that.

To Victor, it meant only one thing: That wasn't Carl he'd been talking to.

7

Hendricks the CEA man showed up at his door the day after the call to Carl, the young man looking concerned. There were two other large, young men with him.

"Sergeant Tremble," Hendricks said.

"Mr. Hendricks," Victor said. "To what do I owe the dubious honor of your company on this fine day?"

"We had some questions come up with your service self-reportage," Hendricks said.

"Lucky Valdez," Victor said. "You're wondering what that is, aren't you? You were monitoring my call?"

"The ACAA monitors every call to Mars, Sergeant Tremble," Hendricks said. "It's more than a national security matter—it's interplanetary security. Who was Lucky Valdez?"

"Nobody you need to know about," Victor said. "It's a private joke between Carl and me."

Hendricks was not pleased with that answer.

"He made no mention of it on his dossier," Hendricks said.

"Yeah," Victor said. "That's why it's a private joke. See, if we put that down on a questionnaire, it wouldn't be private anymore, now, would it?"

Hendricks tried to soften his bearing, tried to manage the veteran across from him. Victor could see the kid trying to do this. The other two men exchanged glances. Victor pointedly ignored them.

"How many people know about this private joke?" Hendricks asked.

"Enough," Victor said. "The thing is, I'm trying to figure out why Carl wasn't in on it. He should have remembered."

Hendricks stared evenly at Victor.

"Your friend is likely having so much fun on Mars these days that he couldn't recall the reference," Hendricks said. "It happens. People are happy on Mars, happier than they were on Earth. Don't you want to be happy, Mr. Tremble?"

"That wasn't Carl," Victor said. "I'm sure of that. It was, I don't know, a simulation of him. Now, I want to know why."

"It hardly matters what you think, Mr. Tremble," Hendricks said. "You're booked on the next flight to Mars. You signed the documents. This means that you're going to Mars."

Victor put his mind to it, thought it through. "What is it? You simulate the colonists? Why?"

"It's expensive to contact Mars," Hendricks said. "It's a cost-saving measure. Simulations are cheap."

"And what?"

"And nothing," Hendricks said. "Mr. Tremble, everything's expensive. Your home's expensive. Your life's expensive. The world's expensive. Mars is terribly expensive."

"Where's Carl?" Victor asked.

"He's on Mars," Hendricks said, gesturing to the two men, who walked over and grabbed Victor, hauling him to his feet. Hendricks put on some sap gloves, something Victor hadn't seen since dealing with insurgents in Frackistan. "You'll see him soon, I can promise you that."

Then he knocked Victor out with a well-placed blow to the head.

8

When Victor came to, he found himself strapped to a chair, a muzzle on his mouth. He was facing forward. There were dozens of other empty seats around him, and a big monitor screen above him. The countdown clock was a bar set at 60 seconds, hovering there in red. He was in an unadorned grey metallic tube—he was aboard the Mars rocket.

Victor struggled at his bonds, but couldn't move. He was in a Type II Interrogation Chair. He'd seen them used in Frackistan. They were light and almost unbreakable. You could beat on a prisoner for days in one, and the chair would take it.

Hendricks was hovering near the entry hatch, then walked in, taking a seat next to him.

"Sorry about that, Mr. Tremble," Hendricks said. "You get the best seat in the house, if that's any consolation. Front and center, Sergeant."

Victor struggled to speak, but the muzzle prevented it.

"We couldn't have you scaring the other colonists," Hendricks said.

Victor's mind was racing, trying to solve for the problem he was facing. Why would they do this to him? What had he discovered?

"They'll be here soon," Hendricks said. "The others, I mean. I don't think you even know what you uncovered, so, I'll tell you, just because you won't be able to tell anybody else. You're not going to Mars. There are no Martian Colonies."

Victor cursed Hendricks from behind the muzzle, feeling his heart go cold.

"There never have been," Hendricks said. "Oh, I know. You're thinking of the trideos, all the shots of people. That's all motion capture technology. All those surveys and such. Everything's staged. Like I said before: space is expensive. You think we'd really grab a bunch of cripples and put them on Mars? Are you kidding? Mars is deadly enough for healthy people, let alone you. No, if God wanted us on Mars, He'd have made it habitable."

Hendricks glanced at his phone, noting the time.

"We're improving America," Hendricks said. "We're getting rid of all of you weak links. Everybody who can't measure up to the President's own Fittest Americans Report. If you fail the FAR, well, then that's that. Eugenics is a dirty word, I know, but we're cleaning up the American gene pool—the AMC is like the net we use to clean the pool. Love it or leave it, right? You're leaving, Mr. Tremble. You and your kind have cost this country enough. So, we're getting rid of you. But this way, there's no trauma—families here at home think their loved ones are on Mars. Even the cripples think they're going to Mars. Everybody's happy. The country gets stronger. We save money not having to spend it on you people. Everybody wins."

Victor fought to free himself, but the bonds were too strong. The chair was purpose-built to restrain him. He'd break before the Type II did.

"This way, you get a one-way trip to the Sun," Hendricks said. "No mass graves. No death camps. No killings, even. Just up you go, off to Heaven. It's euthanasia, really. Disability payments cease. We're doing you a favor, when you think about it. Everybody left behind here on Earth, well, we're happier, we're sure as hell healthier, and there's more for us to enjoy, without you draining our resources. The program has been a huge success—I mean, people actually think we're on Mars. We picked areas where telescopes couldn't spy on us—that's where the pretend AMC is. Oh, and here's the best thing: once get ship the last of you to the Sun, after a few years, we're going to 'discover' a plague on Mars, and you're all going to die out, anyway. We're going to have to quarantine the planet. Isn't that perfect? This way, instead of being a drain on our country's finances, you get to die heroes."

Hendricks' phone chirped, and he smiled, while Victor cursed him out behind his gag.

"No need to thank me, Mr. Tremble," Hendricks said. "You're doing your country a great service. Other countries are doing their own thing—China's got a eugenics program. India's got their own space race going. They know the score. They know what we're doing, and they approve of it. They have their own undesirables. We're trailblazing, here. Anyhow, good luck, and God Bless, Mr. Tremble. The others are coming. Normally, I wouldn't go to this kind of trouble for a candidate, but I know you'd want to know."

Hendricks disappeared, and Victor cursed him. It was all a colossal sham. How had nobody uncovered this before? Or maybe they had, and Hendricks and his type had killed them.

He saw other "colonists" boarding the rocket, proudly wearing their ACAA uniform jumpsuits, which matched his own. He saw Melanie board, who, seeing him, brightened, bounding over to sit next to him. Their hope and excitement made Victor cry.

"Hi, Victor!" Melanie said, waving at him and noting the bonds that held him fast. "Isn't this exciting?"

Victor felt tears running down his cheeks as he fought to speak, fought to free himself. What would happen? Would he be a fugitive? Would they shoot him down? First order of business was getting free. But there wasn't any way out of a Type II Interrogation Chair. Made with pride in the USA.

"Mmmmph," Victor said.

"I know," Melanie said, patting his arm. "Although, why did they lock you up like that? Are you scared? It's going to be alright. Everybody has anxiety. This is no different."

The seats filled around them, as support staff helped the various colonist-victims aboard, securing them in their seats. The support staff wore white suits, and their faces were all cold masks of fear, solemnity, and sorrow. They were people putting a brave face on a horrible thing. Victor could see it. How could people sign on for this kind of detail? Maybe they were threatened with death, too. Anything was possible.

"I had dreams of Mars last night," Melanie said. "I didn't think I was going to sleep, so I took some anti-anxiety medication. Affirmitol. It's so, so good. I hope they have it on Mars. It works wonders. Do you think they have Affirmitol on Mars? They wouldn't let me bring any with me for the trip."

She looked at ease, comfortable next to him. The white-suited handlers were helping the blind colonists to their seats, a whole row of them, more than he'd seen at the training. The handlers seemed to know who Victor was, kept glancing at him to be sure his restraints were holding. Their eyes showed their own fear. They looked like walking corpses to him. Victor thought about the 25 million so-called Martian colonists. Had these walking dead shipped them all out? Or did the ACAA sort through its handlers, too? He was sure they had a system worked out for it. Maybe there was incentive pay.

"I thought I might take up painting on Mars," Melanie said, glancing at her fingernails, upon which had been painted playful unicorns capering on a field of pink. She had a whole herd of unicorns at her fingertips. "I know that's probably hard to do, like in terms of supplies. But if I could access some Martian pigments, I think it might work. Then, maybe I could sell them back on Earth. I haven't worked out the details, yet. I could become the first artist on Mars."

"Mmmph," Victor said, watching the last of the seats get filled with a trio of people with some kind of neuromuscular disorder. They were getting strapped in, too.

One of the handlers checked Victor's restraints. Victor tried to say something to her, to beg his way free of this.

"Mmmph!" Victor said.

"I'm sorry, Sergeant Tremble," the handler said. "Orders are orders. I'm just following orders, here. You'll be happier on Mars."

She glanced at Melanie, who smiled at her, uncertain at what she was seeing. The handler choked out an ashen smile at Melanie, before clearing the room. She was a young woman, pale as milk, like a ghost. Her ID patch identified her as Mallory, but Victor was unsure if that was her first name or last name. It didn't matter.

The excited chatter of the other victims was almost more than Victor could bear. He wept. This wasn't how he'd imagined it going for him. He'd actually hoped to see Mars, to see Carl, and maybe their other friends. For a moment, he'd had hope. Hope was beautiful. But there was no hope here for him.

Mallory shut the hatch, and the countdown clock began counting down after another minute, and Victor could hear the excited victims counting it down, Melanie grinning.

When it got to ten seconds, the rocket began to shake and rumble, and the others got even more excited, as the rocket was hurled at high velocity by the railgun. There was nothing like it, that dizzying sensation of breaking the bounds of gravity. Victor felt the ecstasy of acceleration, his body responding to it, despite his terror and rage. He'd never considered the space program, but could, for a split second, feel the wonder of it.

Several of the passengers had apparently passed out. Many of them were scared. Victor was howling, while Melanie, her hair a gravity-free nimbus around her, laughed.

"I feel queasy, but I don't entirely mind," she said. "It feels so weird."

The rocket fired, and gravity reasserted itself, slamming everybody back into their seats. Then the monitor display sprang to life, filling the cabin with the well-tanned face of President Biff Dixon.

"My fellow 'Muricans," Dixon said. "You are among the last of the 25 million brave souls who are heading to Mars. I want you to know, on behalf of the 'Murican people, that we appreciate your great sacrifice. Because you were chosen to represent us on Mars, the rest of the country is able to live better."

Victor could see flashes in his eyes every time he blinked, the cosmic rays lancing through them. Others exclaimed in wonder and delight. Victor wondered if they even bothered with radiation shielding. He doubted it. Too expensive, right?

"When God asked Abraham to sacrifice his own son, you all know what Abraham did. He went and did it. Almost. He was willing to, though. And that's the important thing. Your sacrifice makes America stronger. You make America stronger. Whether you're here, or on Mars. You're bringing American values with you, wherever you go."

Victor had no idea how rapidly they were traveling, but remembered that the Earth was 93 million miles from the Sun. If they hadn't bothered with radiation shielding, there was no way they'd bothered with life support. In short order, people would begin to suffocate. The rocket would become a ghost ship, to be incinerated by the Sun. Some digital ghost of him would remain, in case somebody called. But nobody would.

Some of them were starting to feel it, the radiation coursing through them, the air thinning. Melanie certainly was, began hyperventilating. Lucky Valdez was having himself a field day, Victor thought, the bitterness exploding in him like the cosmic rays that were perforating his body.

"God Bless You. And God Bless the United States of America," Biff Dixon said, as his flickering face dissolved, a massive American flag began waving on the screen, and the "Star-Spangled Banner" played, prompting the victims to sing along, nervously, their voices wavering, plenty of them coughing and wheezing. Victor closed his eyes, while Melanie was having a panic attack next to him, gasping, flailing, and wailing.

It was getting harder to breathe by the second, but so many of them still tried to sing.

A NOTE ON THE TYPE

The text of this book is set in Minion 3, an updated and expanded version of Robert Slimbach's iconic text typeface. The first version of Minion was released in 1990 and is inspired by classical, old style typefaces of the late Renaissance, a period of elegant, beautiful, and highly readable type designs. Minion Pro combines the aesthetic and functional qualities that make text type highly readable with the versatility of OpenType digital technology, yielding unprecedented flexibility and typographic control, whether for lengthy text or display settings.

Robert Slimbach, who joined Adobe in 1987, began working seriously on type and calligraphy four years earlier in the type drawing department of Autologic in Newbury Park, California. Since then, he has concentrated primarily on designing text faces for digital technology, drawing inspiration from classical sources. In 1991, he received the Prix Charles Peignot from Association Typographique Internationale for excellence in type design. Slimbach now directs Adobe's type design program.

The story titles and subheadings of this book are set in Futura PT Condensed, by Paratype. Futura was designed for Bauer company in 1927 by Paul Renner, and is a sans serif face based on geometrical shapes, representative of the aesthetics of the Bauhaus school of the 1920s-30s. Issued by the Bauer Foundry in a wide range of weights and widths, Futura became a very popular choice for text and display settings.

Composed by Clever Crow Consulting and Design
Pittsburgh Pennsylvania

ACKNOWLEDGMENTS

I would like to thank Christine Marie Scott of Clever Crow Consulting and Design in Pittsburgh for her wonderful cover art and her invaluable assistance with the layout and design of these pages.

ABOUT THE AUTHOR

Born in Missouri, growing up in Ohio, and settling in Chicago, D. T. Neal has always written fiction, but only got really serious about it in the late 90s. He brings a strong Rust Belt perspective to his writing, a kind of "Northern Gothic" aesthetic reflective of his background.

Writing his first novel at 29, he then devoted time to his craft and worked on short stories, occupying a space between genre and literary fiction, with an emphasis on horror, science fiction, and fantasy. He has seen some of his short stories published in "Albedo 1," Ireland's premier magazine of speculative fiction, and he won second place in their Aeon Award in 2008 for his short story, "Aegis." He has lived in Chicago since 1993, and is a passionate fan of music, a student of pop culture, an avid photographer and bicycler, and enjoys cooking.

He has published six novels, *Saamaanthaa, The Happening,* and *Norm*—collectively known as The Wolfshadow Trilogy—*Chosen, Suckage,* the cosmic folk horror-comedy thriller, *The Cursed Earth.* He has also published three novellas—*Relict, Summerville,* and *The Day of the Nightfish.*

ALSO BY D.T. NEAL

THE WOLFSHADOW TRILOGY
Saamaanthaa
The Happening
Norm

Lupinia:
The Selected Poems
of Polly Drinkwater, 2007–2015
A WOLFSHADOW BOOK

NOVELS
Chosen
Suckage
The Cursed Earth

NOVELLAS
Relict
Summerville
The Day of the Nightfish

COLLECTIONS
The Thing in Yellow

Nosetouch Press is an independent book publisher
tandemly based in Chicago and Pittsburgh.
We are dedicated to bringing some of today's most
energizing fiction to readers around the world.

Our commitment to classic book design in a digital
environment brings an innovative and authentic
approach to the traditions of literary excellence.

*We're Out There™

NOSETOUCHPRESS.COM

Horror | Science Fiction | Fantasy | Mystery
Supernatural | Gothic | Weird

9 781944 286316